I0760290

DRAGONFLY

ALYSSA THIESSEN

Peasantry
PRESS

Printed in the United States of America

This title is also available as an e-book. Visit www.peasantrypress.com for information.

Information requests should be addressed to info@peasantrypress.com

Cover Design: Peasantry Press
Skyline Image: DarkCity - kiim.net

ISBN 978-1-988276-05-2 (hdcvr.)
ISBN 978-0-9940210-0-7 (pbk.)
ISBN 978-0-9940210-1-4 (e-bk.)

PEASANTRY PRESS
Winnipeg, Manitoba, Canada
www.peasantrypress.com

To my children

1

It wouldn't be long now. Sitting atop the gray skyscraper with my feet dangling carelessly over the ledge, I was concealed by the dark of the early evening. They existed down there, sure, but up here, it was just me and my marks. People were fools, generally speaking. They believed in only what they could see in front of them, or what they were certain existed above or below. Who was I to complain? If they were a little more observant, maybe less arrogant, my life wouldn't be nearly as successful. Fools were great for business.

I exhaled, watching the thin white cloud of my breath appear and then dissipate. I wondered, somewhat morbidly I supposed, what it would feel like if I shifted too suddenly, lost my balance, and didn't stop myself. What would it feel like to simply – fall? Would I try to catch myself, would I cry out – or would it be like this moment – so completely, perfectly peaceful? I held my breath. If I could have stopped time, I would have then. Just frozen the whole thing. Nights like this had held a strange comfort for me lately. At eighteen, the darkness was the closest thing I'd ever had to a romance. Its cover was almost a caress. Letting my lungs deflate in a rush, I blinked the thought away. The evening was passing and it would soon be time to make my move.

I raised the binoculars to my eyes and peered through. I'd done it so often they almost felt like an extension of my fingertips. The man in the high-rise condo across from me was putting on his black suit coat, with that easy, familiar motion exhibited by every wealthy, faceless mark I'd chosen this month. His wife was generic. She'd be glued to him all evening.

Of course, I'd be long gone before they walked back through that door, and their wall safe would be substantially emptier. They wouldn't even notice its absent contents until next week Wednesday when, as I'd observed for the past three weeks, he would deposit into it a large amount of *emergency* cash, along with some personal items of which his wife would undoubtedly prefer to remain unaware. I was only interested in the cash.

As I waited for them to leave, I watched the usual dance take place, swinging my feet to its silent rhythm. It was the game echoed in relationships just like theirs all over the city, all over the country, and, as I'd observed on many occasions, in a number of subtle and beautiful ways, all over the world. She stood in front of the mirror and straightened her bangs. She toyed with her lipstick, slowly and carefully applying the final coat of a deep red on her thin lips. And she still had to curl her lashes. He cleared his throat from the doorway, shuffling his feet, waiting with his hand on the knob. Although, in most ways, she lived for him, she seemed to exert what little control she had by making him late.

Their limousine pulled up – I recognized it from two nights prior when they had attended an art gala for a client – and they would soon make their way down. Stretching my long legs straight in front of me and my arms over my head, I looked up into the clouded, starless sky and counted the hours until the sun came up and stole my freedom. For now, the height of my perch and the color of night made me invisible to the people below and around me. I didn't need the light to see. It was one of the few perks of being me.

When I was going through a stage last year, I spent an inordinate number of nights in darkened libraries. I read everything I could find about flying people. Books about beings with white, feathered, angel-like annexes – eagle men. I read one story about a girl with reptilian wings that were scaled and sharp and fire red. Some writers imagined the ability to fly came with extraordinary speed or unparalleled strength. Maybe if you were Superman, it did. If you were Joshua Miller, it only came with a set of four translucent wings, a love of the cold, night vision, and the inability to sleep comfortably on your back.

Finally, the suite was empty. As the limo pulled away, I took the tight black balaclava out of my pocket and pulled it over my head. Unnecessary, since my face wasn't the problem, but it was a habitual precaution I'd always taken. I figured it made me look more intimidating, with my dark eyes peering out of the black mask, than being seen with my fine features and nearly black hair. Other than the wings, there was really nothing memorable about me at all.

Stepping to the ledge, I fought the urge to jump. Patient. Steady. I slowed my breath. Some people, those ridiculous beings terrified of high places and breathtaking beauty, would never experience the pleasure of the view from up here. I lived for it.

The limo's brake lights flashed once as the car slowed and disappeared around the corner. I watched the empty space, and then, looking forward, stepped off the edge.

Instinctively, my wings caught the air on their downward stroke, the current lifting me level with the window, my body tilted forward at a 40-degree angle. I imagined any other type of wings would carry me through the sky like some sort of angel. Instead, my insect-like wings forced me to fly more like a bug than a heavenly being. It was fitting, I supposed, considering my line of work.

I approached the balcony cautiously. The neighboring

apartments were occupied, after all, and I'd made the unpleasant discovery in the past that the sight of my winged self would not be well received, despite my efforts to make them seem artificial. Every time I flew, I attached a series of straps and harnesses and I fastened a remote to my waist. I thought it looked pretty convincing, myself, and I imagined it would be enough to fool the public, should a photographer get a lucky shot, but, for the most part, people tended to ignore the straps and focus on the wings.

Landing, I stepped forward and cupped my hands tight around my eyes, peering through the darkly tinted window. There would be no one inside, but I hadn't survived this long by being careless. Other people my age were just finishing high school. I was an expert in break and enter.

I opened the unlocked door and stepped inside. People were ridiculously confident that they were unreachable in their high-rise apartments and expensive condominiums. With my four wings tucked tightly behind me, I made my way through the spacious living room. An ornate crystal vase adorned the shelf, with four crystal angel figurines below. I had no doubt that they were genuine and I resisted the urge to pocket one. They'd be worth a fortune, but fencing them would be next to impossible for me. How did that expression go? Cash is King.

In the kitchen, I ran my gloved fingers along the surface of the marble countertop. It was beautiful. Cold. Clean. A small island stood in the center, between the counter and the large stainless steel fridge. I opened the fridge, knowing what I would find there: expensive champagne, exotic fruit, various brands of bottled water. Luxuries. I grabbed a single purple grape and closed the fridge. Popping it into my mouth, I continued toward the safe. I had time, but not all night. Once there, I didn't hesitate. I entered the combination I'd seen the man do twice before. After a quiet click, the lock released; I turned the handle.

I slid the cash out and into my satchel. It wasn't just easy; it was perfect. I closed the safe, spun the lock, and left the way I had come. When I was still learning, I spent more time getting to know my marks, trying to understand them, trying to imagine what it would feel like to have their families, to actually love something enough to make it worth losing. I didn't waste my time wondering anymore. In fact, this time I didn't even glance at the bedroom as I left. Soon, I was on the ledge and, then, in the air, pulling off my mask and tucking it into my belt.

I let my wings carry me high over the buildings that decorated the city skyline. I took my time, savouring the wind whirling around my wings and flowing over me. Daylight would come soon enough and imprison me in my apartment. I was in no rush to get back. I made my way through the night sky, down past the towers and the offices and the houses, to the edge of Central Park. As I landed beside a small cluster of trees to wait for Marcus, I tucked my four wings in close to my body, the top two pulled downward to rest on the bottom two.

Sometimes I threw on my flimsy, black trench coat after I landed. Not that it did a great job of hiding the wings – the tips extended to less than an inch from the ground – and anyone paying attention might notice them protruding from the bottom. I was pretty sure casual observers wouldn't really be studying my feet though, and I was almost certain they wouldn't attribute my misshapen back to hidden wings. I'd thought of getting something heavier, something that would pull the wings in tighter and hang lower, but putting weight on the wings when they were folded was painful. They were made for flight.

Tonight, I didn't bother with the coat. I wouldn't be long, and Marcus was familiar with the sight of them. The shuffle of the man I trusted most – in this city, at least – rustled the grass just off the main walkway. He cleared his throat, signalling to me. I stepped out from the darkness, just past the tree line, leaving my wings enshrouded by the leaves.

He grinned, his yellowed teeth barely visible by the park lamplight. "I brought you the food and stuff you asked for, Kid", he whispered, almost too softly to be heard.

"Thanks." I took the bag from his hand.

"No problem." His pupils were dilated and his gaze darted around quickly, looking into the trees, then down the path, then back into the darkness. "You can count on me."

"I know," I said, already shaking my head at him as he predictably held out my change to me. "You keep it. A gift." He nodded vigorously, shoving the handful of bills into his pockets. Most of my contacts were happy with a fee-for-service arrangement, but Marcus didn't want to feel like his silence came at a cost. He was under the impression that there was a great government conspiracy to the way I was, that this secret that he'd agreed to keep was thwarting The Man's dark plans. He didn't realize that keeping the secret had nothing to do with the government.

"So, how'd it go?" he asked, his voice still in a low whisper, his eyes still a little too wide.

"It was good," I said. "Perfect."

"Did you get that project done?"

"Yep." I never gave details, and he never asked for them. I didn't want to complicate things. In reality, I preferred that nobody know anything about me at all. Meeting my practical needs, however, required some trust. And I could count on people like Marcus – people who had already learned that the world is a dangerous place and that nobody can really be trusted at all, people who nobody would believe anyway, if they decided to sell me out.

"How about you, Marcus? How are the kids?

"Good, good. Jenny started preschool today. She looked beautiful, with her hair in red ribbons and her pink sundress on."

I nodded. "Bet she was excited."

"She was. And Kevin, he took his first steps today. It was amazing." He laughed now, loudly, startling both of us, and then lowered his voice again and whispered, "I've never seen anything like it."

"Sounds like you have a really nice family."

"I do, I do." I'd heard about Jenny's first day at preschool and Kevin's first steps at least a dozen times since I'd met Marcus. I could recite the stories by heart. The children never aged. I wasn't sure if he'd constructed them out of a fantasy or if they were part of a distant memory. Whatever the truth, it didn't matter. Already he'd begun the familiar story of his wife's tears as she'd waved goodbye to the little yellow bus as it disappeared down the street. It would have made me sad, if I'd let it. I sometimes thought it would be harder to have had something like that and then to have lost it than not to have had it at all. I wasn't really sure, though, that Marcus realized he'd lost anything. It was better, I imagined, if he didn't.

He handed me the bag, looking up in the sky now. Marcus, despite his loose grasp on reality, was always keenly aware of my need to be invisible when the sun came up. I watched him, his expression alight with a level of concentration that normally was nonexistent. His eyes flickered again to my face.

"Better get goin', Josh," he whispered, more urgently than necessary. "You don't wanna be caught out here in daylight." I nodded and took a few steps back into the dark of the woods. "I'll see you next week if you haven't left yet. Wednesday, right?"

"Yeah, Wednesday, if I'm still in the city. Same time, about." Fresh fruit never lasted very long. A week was easy to plan for. Besides, I never knew how long I'd be around. "See you, Marcus." I didn't wait for a reply.

2

Daylight found me alone in an abandoned apartment downtown. Marcus was reliable, but he wasn't the type of person who could take my cash and turn it into a swanky hotel room. Some contacts could and did, but not Marcus. I didn't mind it. Places like this suited me sometimes. Less likely to have housekeeping knocking at my door, anyway. And he'd managed to furnish my room with an old green couch that was comfortable enough and a small, legless table, built up with stacks of newspapers. If that wasn't friendship, I didn't know what was.

I sunk into the couch to count my take. A good haul – there would be no worries for a long time. There hadn't really been any worries for a while. I'd perfected my craft so I would only need two or three marks a month. I rolled the money up in the t-shirt, with the rest, and placed it in the low, loose tile above my head.

Lying on my stomach with my wings pulled in behind me and my hands tucked under my chin, I stared at the daylight glinting through the open blinds. What were they all doing out there? I used to go out during the day, especially in the countryside, in remote areas. It was fine – perfectly safe when nobody was around. But now, the light seemed garish. Everything was uglier in the honest rays of the sun. I read, once, that the bright oranges and fiery reds and deep pinks of sunrise light up the sky, but all I ever saw in the sunrise was a world in which I had no interest in being a part. I closed my eyes against the light and, as it always did, sleep found me.

The cold quiet of night descended subtly. Slowly I rose from my prone position and curled my toes under me, enjoying the textured grain against my skin. It was dusk. Time to go.

I changed as quickly as possible, given the awkward nature of my wings. I'd often thought of modifying my shirts beyond the two long slits running the length of the back, but I nearly had the process down to a science by now. I positioned my wings downwards, forced each pair through the slits of the inside-out t-shirt, and then pulled the fitted black shirt up past the wings and against my body. I righted it as I pulled it over my head. Not that it mattered if it was inside out, I guessed, but if I was going to do something, I wanted to do it well.

I replaced my black pants with identical ones. The air would be cold but, for whatever reason, my body ran at a higher temperature. I never minded the cold. I wrapped the artificial strap system around me and hoped that it looked convincing, at least passably so. I pulled my mask on, and climbed out of the screenless window and onto the fire escape.

My first marks this evening weren't far from my last, but I would have to move quickly. I landed on the rooftop across from their oversized apartment. Sitting, I watched them through the large, rectangular window in their living room. They were moving quickly, and in practiced fashion, through the rooms of their suite that spanned the entire floor. These people were as predictable as always, an endless parade of deadlines to meet and lists to accomplish, so intent on their next destination that they didn't really stop to think about their present. They didn't, for instance, look out their enormous window and see me perched up on the opposite roof, watching them through my binoculars. Of course, had they looked, they may have only noticed a slight shadow, insufficient to convince them they saw anything at all. But, the thing was, they never looked. I could always count on the blindness of the wealthy.

The husband slid his tie tight in a smooth, practiced motion. The wife patted her hair, and her son, who seemed a little young to enjoy this type of thing, laced up his patent leather shoes and licked his thumb to wipe off a small scuff near the toe. The daughter, I noticed, had changed her hair color again. It was bright red now. I seemed to remember it being blonde two nights ago and a sort of a purple the week before that. I couldn't tell how old she was – definitely mid or late teens – sixteen, maybe. Not much younger than myself, in physical years. Much younger, I could almost guarantee, in life experience. If we measured age by our choices, I would be far older than anyone in that place. I watched her slide on her pumps and wait by the door with her father and brother. Of course, her mother had one last stop to make in the bathroom. She'd forgotten, I could imagine her saying, to apply her final coat of lipstick or to straighten that little strand of hair escaping from her bun in the back. I didn't know what excuse she'd made, but I wasn't surprised to see them waiting. I shifted my attention to the bathroom door.

They almost had me fooled, the first few times I watched them. But they were empty, like the others, trying to manufacture family by ritualizing one night of togetherness. Here it was, Thursday again, and they'd be leaving in the Bentley precisely at 6:15. They'd come back no closer to one another than when they left. Not that it mattered to me. Once they were gone, I hoped to be in and out in moments.

When the woman emerged, she grabbed her handbag from the small table by the front door and looked around, her lips pursed. They'd left without her. I allowed myself to grin slightly. She quickly checked for the house keys one last time, and then she left as well. They were off now, and I was on. I reminded myself – patience. But I felt the relentless pressure of time passing. I didn't know exactly when they'd be home, and there was still the other mark to get to. If I didn't go now, I'd need to wait a whole week, and I was anxious to move on. It was never a good idea to stay in one place, and my time here was already dragging. Looking down at the street, I waited for the father's Bentley to pull out of the parkade. The white high beams, lighting up the darkened street, indicated his exit. I let my wings carry me across the road, above the dot-like cars, and to their waiting window. They didn't have the luxury of a balcony, but they didn't suffer for it.

Having no balcony, of course, was less convenient for me, since balconies almost always meant unlooked doors. Over the years, though, I'd gotten pretty good at removing window screens and sliding the glass open. I carried the necessary tools with me, shoved into my pockets, although I rarely needed them. I entered the room quietly. As always, I made my way through the apartment, heading for where they hid their cash.

A slight noise behind me stopped me dead. I turned, startled, and met the very wide, very green, very frightened eyes of the girl. She was sitting on their white leather couch, her feet curled under her, the remote clutched tightly in her fist. Her eyes were darting from my wings to my face to my gloved hands and back to my face again. I *knew* with complete certainty that I needed to leave, but my body was not responding. "Please, don't." Her voice was small, almost a whisper. I could hear fear etched in every syllable. "Please take whatever you want. Don't hurt me." I shook my head quickly and, without thinking, pulled off my mask so she could see my face. *Leave. Just leave.* Again, though, I stayed where I was. I imagined her heart was beating furiously. Like mine. In all the time I'd been making my living from careless, busy, predictable wealth, I'd never been caught. I'd never been confronted. I'd never even thought of deliberately showing my face. And I'd never felt as alive as I did at that moment. I could hear the sound of my heart thundering in my ears, and I wondered vaguely what I would do if she made a dash for the phone. Would I leave? Would I try to explain myself? Would I snatch it from her hand? She didn't move though. She simply sat, waiting. Waiting for me to tell her what I wanted. Waiting for me to go. Waiting for me to *do* something. I cleared my throat.

"I'm sorry." My voice was strange in my ears. "I'm not going to hurt you…" I shuffled silently through the possible explanations. They all sounded equally bad. Instead, I gestured feebly to the bag at my waist. "It's how I make a living," I said, shrugging slightly, uncomfortable. "I didn't think you'd be home."

"I told them I wasn't feeling well." She sounded a little defensive and, although still fearful, she seemed calmer now. We remained like that for a moment, a strange moment, and then she asked, "Are they real?"

I knew what she was referring to, and I tried to be believable. "No." I laughed then, and it was genuine, a release of the anxiety and surprise and fear and excitement caused by my first real contact with an ordinary, stable human being – a female human being. At least the first contact I could remember having. Somebody obviously raised me, and there was always a woman in the fuzzy memories I managed to pull up. Aside from the vague memories though, most of the past was a blank.

"I made them," I told her, and I knew I seemed convincing. I'd practiced this, but it was the first time I'd actually gotten to perform. "They're wire, mostly. And a thin mesh. And I attached them," I said, gesturing to the straps around my body, "with these. There's a thin motor under my shirt, running the wings. Remote control." She nodded, looking fascinated in spite of herself.

"If you invented that, why would you have to make your living like… this?"

"It's more exciting," I told her, improvising. "And getting something like this patented is more difficult than you'd think."

"Mmm." She shifted her gaze back to my face. "How old are you? Don't you have parents?"

"No. Wait, what?"

"How old…"

"No, I heard you." This conversation was throwing me. "Eighteen. I think I'm eighteen."

"You don't know?"

"No." I knew it was definitely past time to leave. I couldn't answer any more questions, and she hadn't called the police yet, so I hadn't had to make a decision about whether or not I would stop her. "Anyway, I should go," I said awkwardly, thankfully remembering to take the remote from my belt and clutch it in my hand as I backed away.

"Goodbye then." She looked like she might smile. Or cry, maybe. She seemed to be as confused as I felt about our exchange. I pulled on my balaclava and turned quickly. I knew her eyes would be on my retreating figure as I climbed through the open window. I glided out, my wings keeping me aloft. I could hear her returning the screen to its frame as I moved through the sky, back the way I came. I didn't stop at the rooftop, and I didn't go to my second mark's apartment. I returned, instead, to my empty home, her wide eyes still clear in my mind. I could feel my heart thumping in my chest. I'd spoken to someone. A girl. And she'd spoken to me. Really looked at me. I wondered, suddenly, if I'd see something about myself in tomorrow's paper. I supposed it was unlikely, because nobody would believe her anyway, but I wondered just the same. I also wondered why I was considering going back again tomorrow. It was crazy enough that I'd talked to her – but going back was suicide.

So I didn't go the next night. Not inside, anyway. Instead, I sat across from her apartment again and watched. I told myself I was simply trying to finish the job. I would find a better time – a safer time. I also told myself I was ensuring that she had kept silent, that nobody there seemed to be acting differently, that no extra precautions were being taken. I spent almost my entire night on the ledge, watching her until my eyes felt dry and my legs cramped. It shouldn't have been exciting.

She watched TV. She lay on the couch and looked at her phone, her fingers busy texting or typing. Mundane, ordinary things I'd watched people do all the time. But somehow, everything about her was fascinating. I loved the way her lips turned up into a smile and parted slightly whenever she laughed. What would it be like to make her laugh?

As the night wore on and the family readied for bed, she stood for a long time at her window and looked out into the night. I knew she couldn't see me, not really, but I wondered if she could see enough to know I was there, that I was watching her. She had to be looking for me. She was looking in my direction, anyway. I peered at her through the binoculars, and I could see her eyes staring back. I thought they'd been green before, but they were brown now. Almost burgundy. Contacts. Or maybe they were contacts before. She was always changing herself, this girl. I realized, with sudden certainty, that I wanted to talk to her again. I wanted to hear her. I didn't want to frighten her or answer her questions; I simply wanted to listen to her voice.

Obviously, I couldn't. How would I even start?

Hi. I'm that guy, you know, the one who broke into your house the other day and stood there like an idiot, staring at you.

Hi, I've been watching your house for the last while so I thought I'd introduce myself.

Hi, I'm…

None of it made any sense. Sitting here, watching her, wondering if she were watching me, didn't make sense either. What made sense was to go home and go to sleep. Or to plan my next job. Or to move on – to go somewhere else. But I didn't want to do any of those things. I wanted to sit here, in the dark, and watch this girl. And I wanted to feel like she was looking at me. Like she could see me.

Eventually, she turned away from the window, and the light in her room went on; I could see the pale glow through the drawn curtains. And then she opened them half way, enough so I could see clearly into her room. She stood at the window again, looking out. She placed her hand on the glass for a moment. What would it be like to be part of that world, at least for a little while? I shouldn't want it; I shouldn't want her.

I packed up the next night. It was definitely time to move on. To go somewhere else, to revisit one of my old haunts in another city, another place. I threw my essential clothes into the small, black duffle bag I carried with me whenever I traveled and I waited until the sky grew dark. I'd come back for the bag after one more flight through the city. Saturday nights were especially risky, as the streets came to life with people and music and light. I wouldn't be long, though. One last look, and I'd be gone.

As I landed in the familiar perch across from her place, I thought I could see the glow from the TV. I watched for about half an hour. There was no movement. What would happen if I went over there? If I introduced myself? And why was I so certain I was about to?

I stood, feeling my wings come to life. They were ready, even if I weren't. I quickly crossed the distance between us and lingered there, at the window. She was alone on the couch, feet tucked up under her, watching television. I knew I was about to do the stupidest thing I'd ever done.

3

I knocked. It seemed more polite than letting myself in, although less so than using the front door. She looked up immediately, as if she'd been expecting me. When her eyes met mine, my hand, which seemed to develop a life of its own, waved slightly. I offered a half-smile. Her move. She sat there, still, for a long moment, and then she picked up her cell and dialed two numbers. I could see her finger hovering over the final number as she came over to the window and, quite surprisingly, opened the screen. "My parents are out. My brother's at a birthday party. You can come in." Her voice was even. "But I'm keeping my hand on the phone."

She moved back to give me room and I wordlessly climbed in. She tilted her head towards the wings again. "Those are amazing. How long did they take you to make?"

"A long time." My voice cracked, and I cleared my throat and shifted uncomfortably. "Years. I guess."

"I knew you'd come back. I don't know how, but I did. I knew it."

"Why did you let me in?"

"I don't know. There's something about you. And maybe I'm bored. I've never seen anything like those things before."

Something about me. "Yeah, they're functional."

"Do you wanna take them off?"

"It'd be complicated to get them back on." That much was true. Not just complicated, of course –impossible.

"Suit yourself." She shrugged and sat on the long couch, crossing her legs in an almost child-like way. As I sat down on the far end, she shifted her body to face me, which made positioning my wings easier. I mirrored her position, allowing my two lower wings to hang off the edge of the seat. "So, you're here now. Name?"

"Joshua."

"You have a last name, Joshua?"

"Miller." It was one of the few things I remembered from before Nik found me.

"Joshua Miller." She said my name slowly, thoughtfully. "Alexa Scott. Lexi."

I had no idea what to say. I went with "hi." The edges of her lips twitched.

"Hi." She allowed herself a quick smile and then assumed again her serious expression. The eye contact was unnerving but I forced myself to return her gaze. "So, Joshua, tell me something about yourself."

"Something about me? Well, I guess you know what I do."

"I know one thing you do, anyway. What else?"

What else? What else was there? I ate alone. I slept alone. "That's not fair," I finally said. "I don't know anything about you." It wasn't exactly true. I knew she coloured her hair as often as some people changed shoes. I knew she wore contacts. I knew she was short and small, like her mother, but had her father's nose, which would have seemed too large for her small, heart shaped face if not for her enormous eyes. I knew her smile seemed to light up an entire room.

"Something about me? Well, my parents think I applied to a bunch of colleges for next fall, but I didn't."

"You've graduated then?" She looked younger than that.

"A year early," she said. Early. I'd never even been to high school. "I'm taking the year off right now and I have no idea what I want to do after. My mom thinks I should take dentistry or something. Follow in her footsteps. Hey, your teeth are really straight."

"Oh. Thanks."

"Ever had braces? I had braces when I was a kid."

"Nope. These are natural." At least, as far as I knew. My memories from my childhood were scattered and vague. I couldn't remember much beyond fragments.

"Well, I had braces for three years. It was embarrassing. I like my teeth now though, so I guess it was worth it."

"Me too."

She frowned. "I thought you said you never had braces."

"I didn't. Have braces, I mean. I meant I like your teeth too." It was an awkward thing to say, but I felt like it was required. And she did have nice teeth.

"Thanks. My dad wants me to be a vet, like him. I volunteer with him sometimes. He has his own clinic," she said, picking up our last conversational thread. "But I think he wants me to follow in his footsteps to impress his friends. His daughter, the animal doctor. And I like it, really. But it's not very – exciting. " Exciting. There was that word again. "What about you? What did you want to be before you became a thief?" Thief. She made me sound like Aladdin. It was nothing like that. It was much more calculated and careful. And I didn't know what else I'd wanted to be. Normal maybe.

"I don't think I ever gave it much thought," I told her. "I don't know if I would be very good at anything else. I'm good at planning. And at being invisible."

She cocked her head and raised her eyebrows, slanting her gaze towards my four large, translucent wings taking up a fair amount of airspace beside the couch. "You? Invisible?"

"Not too many people are out, looking up at the sky at night. Not in a city like this. In the country, maybe, with the stars, but then it's so dark. And here, people are looking at each other – eye-level. And besides, I dress in black. And you can't really see the wings, you know, when it's dark out. These things are almost see-through, right?"

"Yeah, I guess so. I guess, though, if they caught the light, you'd notice them."

"Right. But, aside from the street lamp lights or lights from the windows, both of which I'm usually above, there isn't really anything to highlight them." She was thinking, I could tell.

"Who taught you to do that?"

"I guess I taught it to myself." It was somewhat true, but not entirely. The woman from my memories and the man with her, I vaguely remembered, had been normal, and I couldn't recall instruction connected to their faces. I wasn't entirely certain if they were my parents, but I felt like they must have been. A man and a woman, in a house somewhere rural, with me, as a child. And fields and animals – maybe a farm. Pieces of memories. I remembered Nik so much better. Nik, who told me the only way I was going to survive was by living unseen, by never staying in one place too long. Nik, who had no wings himself, who taught me how to use my abilities to survive, to be better than all these people who called themselves normal. To use them without their ever knowing about me.

"So?" she asked. "What do you do? For fun? I mean, besides the whole break-and-enter-thing."

"It's not exactly –" I thought about how I could explain. "It's not like doing that is exactly – fun." I hesitated. Maybe it was. Maybe the watching, and the meticulous planning, and the knowing exactly what people were doing and exactly where they would be at exactly what moment was the closest thing I had to a good time. It couldn't be all I did for fun, though. "Well, I go flying. Obviously. I take the wings up, you know. All the time."

"Sure," she said, and then her eyes lit up, and I knew exactly what she was about to ask. "Do you think you would let someone else try them? Like, if you showed me how, do you think you would ever let me take them out?" I was starting to figure this girl out. She was looking for something. I would disappoint her, I knew. I didn't even know if I could carry another grown person. I'd tried to lift someone once – Nik. He'd been far too heavy to even get off the ground, but I was younger then – barely twelve, he told me, when I met him, which made me about fourteen when he was gone. I'd been alone for the last four years. But, of course, she wasn't asking if I could lift her. She was asking if I could lend my wings to her, and that, definitely, wasn't an option.

"I designed them to fit my body specifically." I couldn't tell if that would satisfy her, so I added, "They're complicated to operate."

"I'm a quick learner. You could teach me. I'd be really careful."

"I'm sorry. I just – I don't lend them out to anyone." There was a truth. "They're the only pair I have. I don't know if I'd be able to fix them if anything happened. So they just – I just keep them with me. If I take them out at all, they're on my body."

"Okay." Defeated. Disappointed. She didn't meet my eyes.

"Maybe, though –" I knew I was about to needlessly lie to her, and I let myself do it. Later, I wondered why I'd made the offer but, deep down, I didn't want her to give up on me. I wanted her to have a reason to see me again. A reason to want me around. "Maybe once we've known each other for a while – you know, when I've had time to explain how they work – maybe then I'll let you use them."

The grin was back. I asked, "So what do *you* do? You know. For fun?"

She cocked her head to one side, thinking. "Lots. I guess I have friends. Call, text, you know." Not first hand, of course. It was difficult to get on a cell plan when you couldn't really let anyone see you. And pointless if you didn't have friends. "And, I hang out with people. Oh!" She sat up, eyes alight. "And I play the guitar. It took me the longest time to convince the folks I was serious about learning. They made me wait until my fifteenth birthday. They gave me my guitar. I started two years ago, and I taught myself."

"And you really didn't take any lessons?"

"Nope. They offered, but I wanted to do it myself. And I think, maybe one day, I'll ..."

"Join a band?" I finished for her.

"No!" She laughed now and touched my forearm briefly. My skin felt warm where her fingers had made contact, and I suddenly found it hard to concentrate. "I was going to say, play for my kids. If I have any."

"Why not..." I was trying to maintain a steady stream of thought. Could a single touch change my world? "Why not join a band, I mean?"

"I'm just not – It's just not how I see myself. I don't like the idea of being in the spotlight. Plus, my parents would freak."

"Are you good?"

"I'm okay. Wanna hear something?"

Did I want to breathe? "Sure." She got up and went into her room, while I tried to collect myself. I tried to think about something other than the soft texture of her fingertips. Impossible. She returned with the guitar. It was a pink acoustic with flower designs along the side.

"Okay. Tell me if you recognize this one." Then she started to play. I closed my eyes, listening to the sound swell and fill the room. Having her play for me was the single most moving experience of my life.

"Recognize it?" she asked. I cleared my throat, slowly opening my eyes. I'd almost forgotten to be listening for the tune, but I'd picked it up at the end. I had to wait, though, for a moment, before I was able to answer.

"I'm pretty sure I've heard it before, although I can't think of the title." I didn't have the chance to listen to much music.

"Brown Eyed Girl," she said. "It was my favorite when I was a kid. My dad used to sing parts of it to me all the time before bed. And I have brown eyes, you know." Today, her eyes were cat-like, jade. "Contacts", she said, gesturing.

"Ah."

"But normally they're brown. My dad has blue eyes. When I was little, he used to sing to me every night. That was before he got promoted. Plus, you know, I'm too old for that sort of thing." She shrugged, seeming to wave away the shadow that briefly crossed her expression. "It's the first thing I learned, though. I played it for him once, and he said he liked it, but I don't think he remembered it from before." She shrugged again. How did it feel to have that kind of childhood memory? Nice, I imagined, although maybe it hurt knowing that something that meant so much to you didn't mean anything to the other person.

"Anyway, that's me." She started strumming again softly. "You don't play any instruments. You fly and steal things for fun. What else is there about you? Where were you born?"

How could I field that one? "I don't really remember." Honesty. How would that go over?

"You don't remember?" I could tell she wasn't sure if she believed me. "You don't remember where you grew up?"

"Not really. Bits and pieces, maybe."

"Kind of like amnesia?"

"Maybe." I shrugged and leaned back against the arm of the chair. She crossed her legs again, resting her guitar across them, and leaned in toward me.

"Do you at least remember your parents?"

"Sometimes. A little, at least. Sometimes I think I dream about them." I sounded weird. But the words were out so I pressed on. "Sometimes, if I smell something or taste something, it will take me back and I think I remember something more. But I don't know. Play me something else."

So she did. Most of the pieces sounded familiar, and I caught snatches of melodies I'd heard wafting through windows and down evening streets. "Don't you sing?" I asked, at one point.

"I do. But I have to know you first."

I wondered, in passing, if that was her hook, her way of keeping me interested. She didn't need one, of course.

I wasn't sure how long we sat there but, when the sound of voices drifted down the hall, outside of the apartment, I stood. My cue to go. She got up quickly and led the way to the window. "Do you have a cell?" she asked. I shook my head in the negative, starting to climb through the small opening. "If I gave you my number, would you call it?" The key was in the lock now; I could hear it.

"Drop it out of the window; I'll catch it." And then I was out and across the street, sitting, waiting for the window to open again. My patience was rewarded when, a few minutes later, a small, white scrap of paper slipped through the side of the frame and fluttered down. I swooped after it, catching it three floors down, and then I headed back up again, the paper clutched firmly in my fingers as if my life depended on it. I didn't look at it, in case it was blank, but sat again, watching. She went into her room, closed her door, turned off the light, and switched on her lamp. And then she stood at her window, looking out toward me, her hand on the pane. She rested her forehead on it first, then turned her head and rested her cheek. I imagined how warm she would feel against the cool of the glass. She went to bed hours before I finally headed back.

Inside, I sat on my couch and unfurled my fist. Crumpled white paper with pink scrawl: ten numbers. Did she really intend for me to call her? Did she believe I would? Would I? And, if I called her, what would I say? Could I ask her to come out with me? Invite myself over? I certainly couldn't invite her over here.

So I didn't call. I did watch my next mark a little. I tried to keep track of his coming and goings. I didn't go by her place at all. I didn't want her to look out of her window and see me watching. I waited, in fact, four days before I couldn't stand missing her anymore.

I finally crept down the back stairs of my apartment building, into the general hallway, and out the front doors. It was two A.M. and, aside from two drunks leaving a bar across the street, there weren't any people who would notice me. I'd thrown on my light trench coat before leaving the apartment just in case.

I inserted the coins and haltingly dialed the numbers she had written. Payphones were getting harder to find, so it felt providential that there was one just outside my place. It rang four times, and then I heard the click. I wondered if she'd dropped the call. It was, after all, the middle of the night and, as I'd observed when studying her family, she was almost always in bed by eleven. "Hi." Her voice was thick, sleep-filled, and I knew I'd awakened her.

"Hi. It's Joshua."

"Joshua?"

"Joshua. Miller. From the other night?" I tried to offer an explanation. "You gave me your number?" There was silence. This wasn't going very well. Did she know a lot of Joshua Millers? Give a lot of people her number? Did she really not remember me?

Finally, she cleared her throat. "You didn't call." Oh.

"I did."

"When?"

"Well, now." There was a beat, and then the phone clicked again. "Hello?" She'd hung up. "Hello?" I asked again, to make sure. I hung up the receiver and stood there, staring at the silent, angry payphone. Did she want me to call back? Voices echoed across the street. People were leaving the bar. I ducked into the apartment and waited for them to pass. Should I go back to my room, forget about the whole thing? Was it an accident? Was she angry I hadn't called sooner? Or had she not wanted me to call at all? After the street was silent again, I waited a few minutes and then, uncertainly, left the safety of the building. I stared at the phone. It would be humiliating to call again and have her hang up. Or not answer at all. I picked up the receiver anyway. Digging in my pocket, I pulled out more change. Last time.

"Hello?" She answered on the first ring. Her tone was clipped.

"Hi. We got disconnected." There was a silence again. "Hello?"

"I hung up."

"Oh." The silence stretched. "You still there?" I finally asked.

"Yes."

I wasn't sure how to respond, although I wouldn't have been surprised to hear her hang up again. I hadn't had any interpersonal conflicts since Nik, and our conflicts were very short-lived. And never quite so awkward.

"I just – I thought I must have imagined you. You didn't call. Why didn't you call?"

"I don't know." Easiest response. She was quiet. "I'm sorry," I added.

"Okay." I could hear the rustling of sheets, and I imagined her getting out of bed to stand at the window. "So, I didn't imagine you then." She still sounded guarded.

"Definitely not."

"Fine." She hesitated, then added, "The family's going out tomorrow." Thursday. "I'm planning to be sick again."

"Okay." I couldn't tell if the conversation were going well or not. Was she inviting me over? "Should I come by at eight?"

"Sure." She was quiet for a moment. Then, "You could come through the front door, you know. Leave the wings at home?"

I wish. "I don't really want anyone to notice me. Plus," I was about to lie again, but this time it was necessary, "I have a job to do an hour earlier."

"Be careful, okay?"

"Always."

"See you later."

I waited until she hung up.

4

I met Marcus later that evening in our spot. He heard me as I moved through the bush. He was waiting for me, with a small plastic bag of groceries in his hand. I was later than usual.

"I was about to go. Wasn't sure if you'd be here tonight." He knew already that, if I didn't show up, it meant I had moved on for the next while. Marcus would, of course, continue to come each week to the park and wait for me, 'just in case.'

"Not heading out just yet. Soon, maybe."

"Good idea, good idea. Can't let anyone get too close, you know. Keep moving. Keep moving."

"I know." I let out my breath slowly, in what probably resembled a sigh.

"Something's on your mind," he said after a moment of silence and no movement from me.

"Maybe. Marcus, I called a girl tonight." I'd never discussed my personal life before. I'd never had one to discuss, anyway.

"A girl? What kind of girl? Where's she from? Why'd you call?" He was on full alert.

"Just – a girl. I met her on a job."

"Um-hum." Not exactly approval. Then, "She pretty?"

"Yep."

"Be careful then." He told me to watch the pretty ones especially. Most pretty girls were trouble. Not his girls, of course; his beautiful wife and sweet little girl were wonderfully perfect. And did I know that his daughter had started preschool that morning?

Before I left, he reached out and touched my arm. As far as I could remember, Marcus had never touched me. "Be careful, Joshua. You don't want to get hurt."

It was too late, though. And it was my own fault.

The next night, across from her building, I glanced at my watch again. 7:55. The family was long gone, but I had resolved to wait until 8:00, and I resisted the urge – again – to go early. I'd been there for almost an hour, waiting. She'd changed three times in the past forty-five minutes. I'd tried not to watch her getting ready, but it was difficult to look away. She was really quite beautiful, although I hadn't noticed it before I'd spoken to her. Watching her now, though, felt like an invasion. Did she know I was out here, trying not to look? Why hadn't she drawn her curtains?

Eight o'clock. I looked around once, but I didn't hesitate long before I crossed the space between us. The large living room window was already open, the screen removed. I climbed in quickly. She was sitting on the couch, watching T.V., pretending that she hadn't been waiting anxiously for me, that she hadn't removed the screen fifteen minutes prior to my arrival, and that she was completely enthralled with this evening's presentation of whatever nature show seemed to be playing, which looked, to me, to be about tigers mating in a sanctuary somewhere – South Africa, maybe. "Hi. Eight, right?" I greeted her as if I were convinced by her pretense.

"Oh," she said, pulling off an exaggerated startle somewhat comically. I struggled to keep a straight face. "You're here. Come in." I was in, but I nodded and sat beside her. "So," she said, glancing sidelong at me, "what do you want to do?" There were many things I could think of, I'm sure, but none that seemed appropriate at the moment. "We could watch a movie." She filled my silence. "We have satellite."

"Sure." A movie. I didn't know if I'd ever watched an entire movie. I'd seen them on before, at my marks' houses. With Nik, it had been all business: the quickest way into a home, the importance of keeping your face covered, the essential nature of gloves. And certainly, there were no movies before Nik.

She was fiddling with the remote now. She located a menu and scrolled through. A movie. Quaint. Surreal, somehow. Watching a movie, with a girl, on a Thursday night. It was such an ordinary, commonplace activity, and yet I had never experienced anything like it. She read me the titles. I wasn't really listening, and I nodded at one she sounded like she liked. It started, and she got up, walked across the room, and turned out the lights. "I'll make us some popcorn," she called, as she went into the lighted kitchen. Popcorn. Whose life was this?

Soon I heard popping; the salty, buttery scent filled the room. The movie had already begun playing, but I was listening to her in the kitchen. The tiny clink of the glass bowl as she took it down from the shelf. The rustling of the bag as she shook the popcorn out. The soft padding of her feet as she walked across the floor to sit down beside me. My upper and lower set of wings were extended on either side of me, flat against the back of the couch, spanning over its entire length. I was certain it was a strange sight, but it didn't matter. Nothing mattered but the sensation of her shoulder touching mine, her arm pressed against the length of my arm, our legs fused at the outside of our thighs. She rested the popcorn on our laps, between us, and I moved my inside hand to rest it on the base of the bowl. She stared at the TV intently.

"Have you seen this before?" I asked.

"Yes." Her reply was quick, a little too shrill. The popcorn sat warming me, but I couldn't bring myself to move my hand to take any. I couldn't remember ever being as aware of another human in my life – and I had spent my life being aware of other humans. I had no idea what was happening on the screen in front of me. I stopped breathing every time she shifted her weight, and I was struck with the distinct knowledge that my right hand, which was resting comfortably on the popcorn bowl, was also resting quite comfortably on her lap. I couldn't think.

I blinked rapidly, trying to get my bearings. I pulled my hand up quickly and reached into the popcorn bowl. The warm kernels gave me something concrete to do, as I focused now on the taste and the texture – anything other than my proximity to her. I suddenly realized, with horrified fascination, that I had turned to watch her bring the popcorn to her lips. I tore my gaze away, fighting to concentrate on the movie, to keep my mind from going places I was unprepared to go. I attempted valiantly to focus on the screen before me. I failed. Miserably. As if they had a life of their own, my fingers found hers within the bowl, and I wrapped her fingers in mine. We sat like that for the remainder of the movie; shoulder to shoulder, thigh to thigh, and hand to hand in the popcorn bowl. As the credits rolled, I hoped there would be no skill-testing question. There had undoubtedly been some sort of plot line of which I should be aware, but I couldn't recall it, not for the life of me.

I was struck by the idea again that I shouldn't be here. Not on some sort of date, with a beautiful girl who didn't know me. Who couldn't ever know me. I turned to her, to tell her I had to leave, to make an excuse. As I met her eyes, though, I was startled to see her watching me intently. Waiting. Waiting for what? Suddenly, some part of me knew. I stood abruptly. "That was good," I told her, my voice forced and too-loud in the intensity of the moment. She looked surprised. The spell was broken. She got to her feet awkwardly.

"Do you want to do something else? We could... I don't know... we could play a game?"

Games. I'd played enough now. "No, I can't," I told her, backing away toward the window. What exactly had I thought I was doing? I thought I could sit with a girl and hold her hand and then what? It wasn't fair. "I have things to do tonight." My wings were at the window now, my hands on the sill. "I should really get going." She looked confused, but I steadied myself and turned my back to her.

"Did I do something wrong?" she asked softly, hurt etched in every word. Her words abruptly halted my retreat. I could no more crawl through that window than take the wings off my back. I sighed, still not looking at her.

"No. It's me. I should never have come. I just –" I hesitated. Simplest answer. Always give the simplest answer. "My life is no good for sharing. A relationship can't work."

There was silence behind me. I felt her move forward to come and stand beside me at the window, at the glass beside the open screen. "Who's talking about a relationship?"

"Lexi, I'm bad for you. You're innocent. Happy."

"Happy?" Her voice cracked. "I'm not *happy*, Joshua. You've spent all this time watching me – and you think I'm happy?"

"You have the whole family thing. Friends. I don't. And I don't want any." *Or I didn't, before I'd met her.* "I don't want to complicate my life."

"Then go. Go if you want to. I don't even know you anyway." Her fingers were tracing shapes along the glass now, in the steam. Swirls, hearts, flowers.

"You're right. You don't know me." I watched her childish art take shape.

"When I saw you, that first time," her voice was small, "I was terrified. But as soon as you took off that mask and let me look into your face, I *wanted* to know you, you know? And then, when you left, I couldn't stop thinking about you – some guy, who broke into my house. I should have been afraid. I should have called the police, or told my parents, or at least hoped you'd never be back. But I couldn't stop watching for you, hoping. So I could know you." I heard her take a shaky breath. "I want you to stay. Joshua, please stay." How could I possibly leave after that?

I captured her fingers in mine now, holding her cold hand against the window. She turned her face to look at me. "I just don't know where this is going," I told her.

"Does it really matter?"

"I guess not. Not really." I imagined pulling her against my body now, leaning in and touching her lips with mine. I could see it vividly, feel it. But instead, I slowly released her hand and let my arm hang down in a semblance of relaxation. I was staying.

I let her take my hand and lead me back inside. We sat on the carpet, in front of the blackened TV. She turned on the light.

The evening passed too quickly. We spent it simply. She made me pasta, told me about her graduation, taught me to play poker. I won every round – I was, after all, a much better liar than she was. At 10:30, the alarm I'd set on my watch began to beep, warning me it was time to go.

"I'd better disappear. Your parents will be home soon."

"You really have been watching." She took my wrist and looked down at the large black watch. "And who wears a watch anymore?"

"What can I say? Tools of the trade. And I'm good at my job." I led the way to the window and then turned, my back against the wall, with her standing just inches from me. I wondered what her lips would taste like. I'd called *her* innocent and naïve, but I'd never even kissed anyone before. I got the distinct impression she wouldn't object. Instead though, I simply nodded and turned to leave.

"Are you really going to call me this time?" she asked.

"Of course." As I disappeared into the darkness, I knew that should be the last lie I'd ever tell her.

It wasn't, though. I called her the next night, and the ones after that. When the streets were dark and abandoned, her natural, soothing alto was an addictive balm to the emptiness. Not that it could last. I knew, ultimately, I'd need to let her go. The longer I waited, the harder it was going to be.

5

Life didn't stop just because I'd met a girl. The mark I'd had in mind when I'd met Lexi was moving. It happened, sometimes, when I tarried too long watching. The family's unpredictable schedules and patterns now, paired with their intended departure, meant I'd need to find a new target and start from scratch. I'd hoped this would keep me busy enough to resist seeing Lexi again.

It didn't. In less than a week, I started to hunger for her presence. Not just because she was beautiful – and she was beautiful, in an uncommon way, with her heart shaped face and ever-changing eyes. But it was her company I ached for.

Of course, I probably would have caved eventually anyway, but it was the kid with the cigarette who did me in. As I hung up the phone that seventh night, before I turned back to my apartment, I noticed a slight movement across the street. A boy – he couldn't be much older than I was – was watching, leaning against the opposite wall, a white cloud of smoke drifting above him. I pulled the long coat more tightly around my wings and hurried back inside. In my room again, I peered out of the window at the stranger. He threw his cigarette on the ground and then looked for a moment at the front door where I'd been. Suddenly, his gaze shifted and his eyes met mine. I stepped back, letting the curtains fall.

I closed my eyes, trying to control my shaking hands. I wasn't easily spooked, but there was something about the way he looked up, like he knew where I'd be. I took a deep breath. If he'd seen me, it was over. I'd have to leave. No more high-rises here. No more Lexi. I looked again, moving the curtain aside slightly. The boy was gone.

It had to have been my imagination. If he'd seen something, he wouldn't have disappeared so quickly. But the close call meant that using that payphone was out. It also meant facing the reality that, sooner or later, I'd have to leave.

It was that fact that found me the next evening at 2 a.m., tapping at Lexi's window, grinning as she came to the window and peered out, and asking her to meet me on the roof.

I circled the rooftop as I waited for her, the false remote clipped on my belt, my extra harnesses, in my hands, for her. Nik had taught me to never do anything without planning meticulously and to avoid any kind of contact. I was about to ignore him on both counts.

Through the dark, the light from the door lit up the concrete pad. I closed in on the rooftop, and I saw her jacketed figure, head tilted up toward me, hands wrapped tightly around her body. I imagined she was shivering. It was a cold night; we were on the brink of winter and, although I was accustomed to being out in the chill, most people were not. She raised her hand in a quick greeting as she saw me appear from the darkness. I landed a few feet from her, easily, comfortably. I'd been doing it all my life. "Why didn't you call first?" she asked, trying to smooth her sleep-teased hair behind her ear. Her light blue nightshirt extended past the hem of her fall jacket, although she'd thrown on jeans underneath. "I would have stayed up."

"The phone I've been using isn't an option anymore."

"Can't you get a cell?"

"It's a risk." Nik had drilled that home. No phone, no trace. Although he'd also insisted no real contact, and I'd obviously completely ignored him. "So," I said, abruptly changing the subject, "have any problem getting up here?"

"None. Everyone's sleeping. And the door wasn't locked – people use the garden up here when it's warmer." She smiled up at me. "I wish you could see yourself flying. It's amazing."

"Yeah?"

"You remind me of a dragonfly," she said. I couldn't help but grin. I'd made the comparison too. "Not just the wings," she added. "The position of your body, the way you move through the air. I love dragonflies. They're beautiful. Everything about them." She looked away now, staring out into the darkness of the night as she spoke. "You know, once, when I was eight, I ran over a dragonfly with my bike. Only the edge of it, but its wings were crumpled and it wasn't moving. I cried and cried and cried. And then I crouched down beside the little thing, closed my eyes, and prayed that God would heal it. When I opened my eyes again, it was gone. No trace."

"Amazing." I managed to deliver the word deadpan.

She nudged me gently. "Laugh if you want. But it was important to me. It showed me that God must care about the faith of a child. Like the things I loved mattered to Him. Because I mattered to Him."

What could I possibly say in response to a story like that? I knew she believed it with everything in her, this tender memory of something she couldn't explain. Her interpretation didn't surprise me – not really. A girl who could ignore the way we met, ignore everything she knew about me and just – accept me anyway – no wonder she believed God healed her dragonfly.

I cleared my throat, smiling lightly. "So, do you want to do this?"

A quick smile darted across her lips. "Without a doubt."

"Okay. We'll see how it goes. I've never, you know, successfully carried anyone before."

"You tried?"

"A few years ago. I failed, though."

"Did she fall?" She was nervous. Good. She probably should be. Maybe she'd change her mind about coming up.

"He. No," I admitted. "I couldn't even get him off the ground."

She hesitated. "You said it was a while ago?"

I nodded slowly. The realization of my error dawned on me, and I groaned, inwardly. Something about her made me forget to lie.

"How old were you when you invented them?"

I tried to think quickly. It was hard to think when she was around. "I was thirteen." Did that sound reasonable? Thirteen? Could someone invent something like this when they were that young – and still manage to keep it a secret?

"And you kept it a secret, that long?" she asked incredulously, echoing my own disbelief in my concocted truth.

I nodded.

"So what? You're some kind of child prodigy?"

"You could say that."

She smiled slightly, then shifted her focus abruptly. "Should I take off my shoes and jacket? To make myself lighter?"

I shook my head quickly. "No, not necessary. It's even colder up there."

"Do you have something to strap us together?" She was smart. I'd thought of that too. That way, if I couldn't hold her, we'd both fall. I held out the harness in my hand to her. This harness wasn't for show, like mine. This one would have to bear her weight. I'd never actually tried it. I hoped that it would do what it was created to do, and if not, that I was strong enough to hold her.

"Ever gone rock climbing?" I asked, as she took the straps.

"Rappelling."

"Know how these go on?"

"Kind of. It was last year. The guide helped us."

"Okay." I moved to help her into it, trying to ignore the fact that I was touching her. I snugged it close around her body, concentrating on keeping my mind clear. I clipped her harness into mine. "We're linked."

That smile appeared again – quick, shy. "Which way will I be facing?"

I'd thought of that already too. She'd have a better view if I held her facing out at the world, but she'd be more secure if she could wrap her arms around my body. "I think that, for this flight, since we're just trying things out, we should start with you facing inward. You could still see if you tilt your head sideways." She nodded quickly. "You need to hold onto me."

"Uh-huh." She nodded again. She stepped closer; her stomach and legs were against mine, and she wrapped her arms around my waist and placed her head on my chest. I held the remote in one hand and then wrapped my arms around her tightly. I was quite certain she could hear the quick, heavy pounding of my heart, and I was hoping she thought its rate was due to anticipation about the flight rather than to her proximity.

Her hair smelled like strawberries. "Ready?" I felt her nod. I took a deep breath. I might not even be able to get off the ground. I wasn't able to with Nik. She was much smaller than he had been, though. I felt my four wings, in response to my thoughts, begin to beat quickly. I could feel their power in a way almost unfamiliar to me. I wasn't a child anymore. Soon we were up, off the roof, hovering above the surface.

We didn't go quickly. My wings weren't usually used for speed as it was and, with her in my arms, I flew even more carefully. And even though the burden of her weight was slight, it did, I soon discovered, take more work.

I could hear her gasp as she noticed the height at which we

flew. She said nothing, and I didn't feel the need to fill the silence with conversation. We flew until my arms and wings began to tire. "We're going to need to go in now," I told her reluctantly.

"K," she answered. Her grip on me loosened, although her body was still tense, and I realized she was weakening as well.

"Should I take you to your window?" I asked.

"Uh huh. I took the screen off for you already." I took her down, along the side of the building, thankful the neighboring apartments were dark. With her in my arms, I wasn't able to thoroughly scan the area. She was making me careless. At the window, it occurred to me that getting her through safely, without the aid of my wings, posed a problem.

"I've got you," I told her, hoping she trusted me enough to follow my instructions. "You'll need to let go of me, though. And unhook yourself." It was a terrifying thing I was telling her to do, but she didn't hesitate. I felt her arms loosen, and then I heard the click of metal as she did as I asked. I shifted her weight and held her out so she could grasp the edge of the window. She scrambled through, and the sudden difference in load made me weightless for a moment. I found myself unexpectedly above the buildings. As I made my way back down, I met her laughing eyes at the window, waiting for me.

"Was I that heavy?" She moved aside to let me crawl through her window. My feet on the carpeted floor, I looked around the feminine room. I'd seen it countless times before, but never from this perspective. It was, as usual, not tidy. Clothes were crumpled in the corner; make-up and hair products and photos lined her dresser.

"You can sit down if you want," she said. I sat cautiously on her unmade bed, marvelling at the smooth texture of the satiny white sheet against my hand. I couldn't help but glance at the crumpled bedspread at my feet. I imagined its cool surface wrapped around her warm skin, and I wondered at my own reaction. *Focus*, I told myself. *Just focus.* She picked up her acoustic guitar and sat beside me, resting it comfortably across her knee and the crook of her arm. Her fingertips caressed the strings, strumming softly.

"Aren't you worried about waking your family?"

"They're heavy sleepers. And when I can't sleep, I play. Plus the door's locked." Then she cocked her head at me, watching me watch her. "It was a pretty amazing ride. So I'll take requests. What do you want to hear?"

"Have you written anything?"

She colored slightly. "Sure. Nothing good, though."

"That's okay. Play me something you wrote. Bet it's better than you think."

"You'd lose that bet. I just mess around a little."

I nudged her foot with mine. "Well, you said it was my request. I want to hear something you wrote."

She nodded slowly. "Okay. But you have to promise to take me up again. Thursday, when my parents are out. You can meet me on the roof."

I nodded solemnly. "Deal." She started with a tune soft and sure; she knew this piece by heart, by feel. And then she started to sing. Her quiet, alto voice rose and fell so softly I had to lean in to hear the words. The lyrics were simple, something about a father and child, and the melody was hauntingly beautiful. When the last note died and she raised her eyes to mine, it took me a moment to realize I'd been holding my breath.

"Wow," I finally whispered. She smiled now, a slow, easy smile. She set the guitar on its stand and settled herself on the bed, her back against her headboard, her feet at my thigh.

"You know what my favorite thing about the night is?" she asked, after a long pause.

"What's that?"

"The quiet. It's so quiet at night."

"Not everywhere."

"No, not everywhere. But here. Up high. Nobody rushing around, nobody fighting. Just – peace. Quiet."

"My favorite time of day."

"I guess you're mostly out at night. With what you do."

"Yeah. It's really the only time that works."

"Think you'll ever decide to do anything different with your life?"

"I don't know. It's really the only thing I'm good at."

She raised an eyebrow. "The *only* thing?"

I looked down at my hands. "I don't think I'm cut out for much else."

"I don't know about that. With an invention like those, you could do a lot of good, I bet." Good. If she had any idea about the violence and injustice I'd watched take place in the world around me, and the coldness with which I'd ignored it, she wouldn't have such high hopes for me. Then again, she had no idea who I really was. "But I guess," she added, "if you didn't do what you do, we'd never have met. And that just wouldn't do, at all." Her voice was soft with sleep now, and I could see her eyelids getting heavy. "The morning after that first time I met you, I wondered if you'd been a dream. But then I knew you must be real. A dream has never... made me feel... the way you do." And then she was quiet, and the room was quiet, and the only sound was the rhythm of her breath. I stood slowly, careful not to disturb the bed, and picked up the comforter from the floor. Laying it gently across her lap, I resisted the urge to kiss her forehead. I'd promised her Thursday but, for the next few days, I needed to focus on my mark.

Focusing was easier said than done. I'd never had problem with my prep work before, although it wasn't like I needed this job to be done any time soon. I wasn't hard up for cash; I had a thick bundle of bills that took up half of my small duffle bag. So instead of memorizing schedules and routines, I caught myself imagining the way her jeans hugged her curves and the rise of color in her cheeks when she laughed. Alone on the ledge, I could have sworn I felt the texture of her fingertips as she wrapped her arms around me, the warmth of her body as she pressed herself against me.

I wasn't a complete fool. I knew there was no future for us, even if I didn't have the wings to separate us. Lexi was too emotionally young, too wealthy, too loved, even if she didn't realize it. Too good. I had no right to see her again. But when did rights ever stop me?

6

As I landed on the rooftop in front of her, she stepped forward and impulsively threw her arms around me. "Hey, Dragonfly," she whispered into my shirt. I held her like that for a moment, close to me, feeling her heart pounding. I hardly recognized myself these days, although I felt more like myself than I had for a very long time. Thursdays had become ours now, and the nights in between, for me, shadows. Each time I came for her, she was waiting, with this same breathless anticipation.

She finally pulled away and looked up at me expectantly. "So, Romeo," she said lightly, changing my title to make me human again, "what's the plan for tonight?" The Romeo reference wasn't lost on me. Nik had had me read and read and read, to ensure I understood the world of which I was a hidden part. Romeo. Part of the thrill of the moment was lost for me. I fit the title of Romeo – love struck, impulsive, foolish. He hurt every person who loved him. I didn't doubt the end of our story would be as perfectly disappointing.

I bowed, forcing my lips into a light smile. "Well, fair Juliet, are you up for a flight this sweet evening?"

"Of course." She clapped her hands together and then laughed.

"I would go flying with you *every* night!"

I didn't reply but busied myself with the straps and harnesses. Since the last time we were up I'd rigged up a better system. Rather than being clipped to my belt and supported by my arms, her harness straps now ran over my shoulders and around my torso, from one side to the other, and then across my chest, so she was actually supported by my body. My arms around her would simply be extra security, not a necessity. It would be a much easier way to fly and it would allow her to face outwards and see the world as I did.

When I told her, her expression fell. "I like seeing your face when we fly," she said. "You should see the look on your face when you're up there."

"No, this time you need to see the world the way I see it. Then you'll know why I have that look on my face." I strapped her in, her back against my chest.

She turned her head partially to look at me. "You know, I still think it would be easier if you'd teach me to use the wings myself."

"Maybe one of these days," I lied. And then we were in the air again, high above the city. I could see through the night easily, almost better than I could in the day. But I knew her night vision was limited to what was illuminated by the stars and city lights. I tried to stay low enough so she could really see the city. I kept my hands around her body, even though it was no longer necessary, because I liked the sensation of my arms around her waist. She had her hands around my arms, and I could tell when she was nervous because she would dig her nails into my skin. I would straighten out or slow down, in response. With the harness like this, it was easier to take her up for a longer period of time. Still,

I wasn't used to flying with another person, and I tired before I wanted to. I reluctantly swung around and brought us back to the rooftop. I had no idea what time it was or how long we'd been up there, although a quick glance at my watch told me it was too long. I unhooked her, and she stood, looking up at the stars. "It's beautiful," she said.

"I know," I said.

"I used to have dreams of flying. I know a lot of people do."

"Yeah?"

"Yeah. And now we don't have to just imagine it. We can actually fly." I turned away from her, walking to the ledge of the building and sitting down, my legs dangling off the edge. I knew exactly where she was going with this line of thought. "Think about how much you could make if you patented those."

I waved her away. "I'm not interested in being rich." That much was true.

"Well, you could patent them, then, and make everyone's life better. Imagine if everyone could fly!" I often did. What would it be like to not have to hide anymore? To be just like everyone else? She came and sat on the edge beside me. I looked down at her feet. Green sneakers.

"Maybe you could use them to help people in another way. You must see a lot from up here." When I didn't say anything, she nudged my foot with hers. "One day, I'll convince you." One day. She was thinking long term.

"I don't think so. You can try, though."

She laughed, her voice quiet in the still night. "I will." Then she leaned her head on my shoulder. How could the impossible feel so right? Everything about it was perfect. About her and about the moment. Everything except me. I was the lie. I covered her hand with mine and she turned her palm upwards. I looked down at our clasped hands.

"I like being here, with you," she said, her words almost lost in the wind.

"Me too."

After a moment, she tapped my foot with hers again. "You know what one of the best things about flying with you is?"

"What's that?"

"Promise me you won't laugh?"

"Nope." I grinned down at our hands.

"Fine. I'll tell you anyway."

"Good."

"It's just – I love it because it feels like we're almost part of the same body. Like we're glued together. Like I'm – a part of you. Inseparable."

"That's the best thing?" I asked her, still teasing. "Flight is wasted on you then."

"Well, it's also pretty up there."

"Breathtaking."

She lifted her head from my shoulder to look at me. "But it wouldn't be as beautiful by myself. Being up there in the sky would be cold and lonely if I weren't with you."

"I'm glad you think so – then maybe you'll stop bugging me about taking them out on your own."

She nudged me with her shoulder. "Nice." She was silent for a moment. Then she asked, "What about you? Do you prefer flying alone or with me?"

"It's much easier to concentrate when I'm by myself."

"That's not what I asked you."

"I've always *been* by myself up there."

"Do I ruin it for you?"

"No. Sometimes I think it's the opposite. Like all flight is kind of ruined now that I know what it's like to fly with you." I could tell she was happy with my response because she squeezed my hand and put her head back on my shoulder.

"That's what I like to hear," she said.

After a while, I glanced down at my watch again. "It's late. I wouldn't be surprised if your family were home and wondering where you are."

"But I'm practically an adult. I'll tell them I went out."

"And they won't mind?"

"They don't really get any say." She had no idea how lucky she was to have someone who thought they *should* have a say.

"Are you disappointed to be missing the family stuff?"

"Not at all." I looked closely at her face. She was being truthful. "When I go out with my family, it's nice. It is. To be with each other. But we don't talk about anything that matters. In fact, we barely even talk at all. We're just – together. And I'd rather be together with you."

I put my arm around her and pulled her close to me, feeling the satisfying weight of her body as she leaned in to me. "I'm glad," I said. Some nights, we'd come down sooner. She'd play for me, or we'd sit together in her bed, just – talking. I wondered more than once if this was what it meant to be truly intimate with somebody. Tonight, though, sitting together on the ledge, was enough.

We sat like that, until the night got very dark and quite cold. I could tell, when I heard her teeth begin to chatter and felt her body start to shake, that it was time to say goodnight. I may have been built for the cold, but she definitely was not. And it was far too cold for her to be out here with such a light jacket and only me for warmth. "We should call it a night. I have some work to do," I said. She nodded and we stood together.

"Be careful out there."

"I will," I said. I wondered what it would be like to kiss her. She was standing so close, her head tilted up, her lips parted. She ran the tip of her pink tongue along her lips, moistening them. I could see myself leaning in and kissing her, and I imagined the taste of her skin, the texture of her lips. I pictured myself touching her hair, running my hand along her neck. But there were promises in such kisses. Even as I leaned in and our bodies touched, I knew there were promises. Instead, I pressed my lips against the cool of her forehead. I felt her sigh. I knew I would go home unsatisfied, but I didn't deserve the brief pleasure her kiss could afford me.

I didn't even really deserve to want her like I did. "Good night, Lexi," I finally whispered against her ear. I held her then, close to me. I knew she could hear the quick rhythm of my heart, and I hoped she understood that she was the cause.

"Good night, Joshua."

With a quick wave, she walked to the rooftop door and, not glancing back, went inside. The door clicked shut and I was alone. I stood staring at it until my fingers stiffened and legs ached. I wondered what it would have been like to follow her, through the door, inside. Impossible, of course. Completely impossible.

7

Later, sitting outside my mark's apartment, it was, as usual, difficult to concentrate on the mundane details of his life. I wanted to be back with Lexi, in her room, listening to her voice and lying next to her. Instead, I was on the cold rooftop alone, watching two nobodies and their money. The husband was, I had already discovered, more or less like the rest of them: wealthy, disinterested, busy, predictable. He was also, however, an unfortunate blend of uneven temper and minimal intelligence, a combination that rendered him unpleasant and volatile most of the time, especially when he was in his domesticity. Although my choice of profession never bothered me, ignoring the violence in people's home used to. Nik had tried his best to condition me to pay no attention to it. Sympathy was a weak emotion and a distracting one, and I couldn't afford to be weak or distracted. *"Never let yourself feel and don't – under any circumstance – get involved."* It had been a long time since watching a scene like the one in front of me had caused me any measure of discomfort.

But watching the man's wife meticulously cover the bruise on her cheek didn't sit right this time, and I was unexpectedly glad he didn't have children. I had to remind myself that the day-today dealings of these people didn't matter to me. At all. People made their own choices, and they themselves, as Nik had said, had the power to change them. Yet I lingered on the form of his wife, sitting in front of her mirror, working with her foundation and blending, blending, blending. I couldn't help but think of Lexi. Would she marry a man like this woman's husband? A pompous, arrogant fool who thought money gave him permission to treat her like she was worthless? Would anyone step in if she did?

As I watched them, night after night, my mood grew darker. The more agitated and angry he was, the more I clenched my fists and paced the rooftop. But what could I do? *I'm no hero*, I reminded myself. *I'm the villain.*

Besides Lexi and my marks, Marcus was my only other point of contact, and lately, the only one I could count on to not play havoc with my emotions.

"Tell her about yourself yet?" he asked, his voice in the usual conspirator's whisper as he handed me the heavy bag of groceries he'd picked up for me.

"No."

"And she hasn't asked too much?"

"She believes what I tell her."

"Then she's too gullible for you. Can't trust a gullible girl," he said with finality. "Gullible girls can't keep your secrets because they trust everyone."

Still mostly concealed by the dark of the trees, I leaned my shoulder against a thick oak and sighed. "Might be true enough, Marcus. But I just can't seem to get her off my mind."

"Mm hmm. Well, be careful."

"Always am." I hesitated again. This conversation was uncharted territory. Was it okay to be talking with him like this? I knew what Nik would have said, but I added anyway, "I like her though." After a pause, I asked, "What was your wife like?" I realized I'd accidentally used the past tense. He didn't seem to notice.

"My wife is great. You should have seen her getting our little girl ready for school this morning. She's a good mom. Beautiful, too. Is your girly pretty?"

"Yep."

"Well, I hope she's a good woman. My wife's a good woman. Everyone should be so lucky." He was blinking rapidly now, worrying his hands.

"Everyone should be so lucky," I agreed.

"Next week – same time. Lay low until then, Kid."

"You betcha."

He was gone. Alone in the night, I wasn't in any hurry to go home just yet. I watched my breath turn white in the cool air. Gullible girls, he had said. I wondered what my own mother had been like. Just shadows of memories. Dark hair, I thought, like mine, and similar eyes to mine: dark brown or maybe even black. My father was even less clear: graying hair, a rough texture on his face – perpetual day-old beard. Not much else. And no wings. I was pretty sure they didn't have wings. I didn't have early memories of flying either, although I was certain I'd always had wings. I remembered being quite young, looking up at a butterfly and feeling my wings respond entirely on their own.

I'd been alone, though, when I'd met Nik. He'd found me in a field somewhere. Cold, like today. My wings had been tucked in tight to my body. All the memories prior to that moment were scattered fragments.

But when Nik reached down and pulled me up, my world came sharply into focus. He'd always told me something traumatic must have happened before he'd found me. He was probably right, considering the fact I was only about twelve years old and alone. When I had no family and no memories and nowhere to go, Nik had given me shelter, taught me a trade, and refused to coddle me. He'd kept my secret, too. I was sure, as a con man and a thief, the thought must have crossed his mind to sell my story, but he never did. He certainly wasn't a father figure, though. Hardened, emotionless, he taught me the things I needed to know. He was the only clear memory of my childhood that I had.

It was time to go. I was starting to get cold, anyway.

Soon, the garish lights ringing in the Christmas season began to appear in the streets below, and the tacky traditional refrains blended with the sounds of the city in a quiet cacophony. The multi-colored glow from the oversized tree that appeared in Lexi's living room, in such stark contrast with my bare apartment, brought a warmth and color to my life I knew I'd never deserve.

"Two days until Christmas," Lexi whispered, sitting on that familiar couch, in front of her big screen TV. Her hand, as always, rested in mine on my lap, her head comfortably on my shoulder. "You've really never celebrated it?"

"Really," I said. "As far as I know."

"I wish you could celebrate with me." And then she asked, after a moment, "Why do we only meet at night?"

I continued to stare blankly at the screen as I thought of an answer that would satisfy her. "I'm not a vampire, if that's what you're worried about." A joke. Not a good one, at that. She was quiet, serious, waiting. "I don't know. With my lifestyle, it's become routine for me to sleep during the day and wake up in the evening."

"But it's not routine for me. Don't you think we could do something in my day? You could take those things off. You could – meet my friends."

Alarmed, I shifted to face her. "You haven't told anyone about me, have you?"

"Well, no. No, not like that."

"Like what?"

"I might have told one of my friends that I met somebody."

I could feel my pulse pounding now. I waited for a moment before replying.

"What, specifically, did you tell her?" I kept my voice even. The anxious look on her face cautioned me to stay calm, stay in control. She was afraid I'd be angry. I was, a little. And terrified. "Lexi?"

"Nothing. Nothing. Just that I – I met someone."

"You said nothing about these?" I gestured to the wings behind me.

She returned to silence, and I groaned inwardly. "I may have said… something." Her cheeks colored and I could see that she was trying not to cry. "I may have mentioned the wings. But only to one friend. We went to school together."

"What did you say, exactly?"

"I said you invented wings. When you were younger," she explained. "She didn't believe me, if that helps. She said I'm always pretending to be something." She gestured to her current dark red hair and purple irises. "She said it was impossible for anyone to make something like that."

"And you want me to meet her to prove that I exist? This isn't enough?"

"It's not like that." Her eyes were wet, and I tried not to care. "It's just – are you embarrassed about me? Or do you have some sort of secret life?"

"Secret life? Like the kind where I fly around on a set of wings at night or the kind where I break into people's homes and steal their stuff?" I wasn't trying to be sarcastic, but I cringed at the tear that traced its quiet way down her cheek and disappeared into the fabric of her jeans. Another one followed it, but she brushed it away angrily.

"No. The kind of life where you have someone else already."

"I have no other life." I sighed, leaned against the back of the couch, and looked away from her out of the window. Just this one.

Just this one where you've suddenly become the only thing that matters to me. Where everything else is just existing.

"So is that a no? To going out in daylight?" I sighed again, unnecessarily loudly. I was in no danger from her friend, I imagined, especially if she doubted my actual existence, but I could never give Lexi what she wanted. If Lexi knew what she were really asking, she would take it back.

"Can we just leave it for now? Keep things the same for the time being?"

"Sure." Her voice was flat. The movie had ended and we were surrounded by silence.

"I should get going. Your family will be here soon." I shifted to get to my feet.

"Hey, Joshua?" She stopped me, her hand on my arm. "I don't know if next Thursday will work so well." Punishing me? For denying her daylight? As if she could read my thoughts, she rushed to explain, "It's just that my dad's getting weird about my not coming out with them anymore. I tried saying that I'm getting too old, but, tonight, he looked sad. He said I wasn't too old, and I should reconsider for next week. I think it matters to them that I'm never there anymore."

I nodded, thinking of my mark, who left purple evidence of his feelings on his wife's body. Lexi was lucky. Luckier than she realized – or maybe she did realize, after all.

"That's okay," I told her. "We'll figure something out." It was a lie. She wanted things from me I could never give her. It was clearer now than it had ever been before. I'd known all along that what we had was impossible. I'd been playing some kind of game, and it had now played itself out. I stood. Could she sense the finality of my response?

"You can call me though," she said, as we reached the window. "We'll think of another time that works." I nodded.

"Be safe," she said, as she always did when I left. I paused at the window and tried to memorize every contour of her face. I traced her jaw line with my thumb. Her skin was smooth and the even tone was natural; she wore no makeup tonight. She put her hand on my shoulder and I slid my hand around her waist. And then, I was kissing her, tasting the sweetness of her mouth and the soft caress of her breath. Hungry in a way I didn't quite understand, I deepened the kiss and then, after a moment, pulled away abruptly. She looked bereft, and I felt it. "See you around," I said, dropping my arm quickly from her body and pulling myself quickly through the window. "And Merry Christmas." I'd forgotten to hold the artificial remote but, from the crushed look on her face, she hadn't noticed.

8

I left her standing there, watching me disappear into the dark, and I imagined her hand pressed against the glass beside the open screen. Her parents would be home soon, so she wouldn't be alone for long. I returned to my other haunt: the familiar perch on the roof across from my marks' apartment. Their Christmas tree was, like most, large and brashly decorated. I'd watched while the wife set it up, the weekend after Thanksgiving. She'd strung the lights alone. Hung the decorations alone. Wrapped the presents alone. When he'd come home, later than usual, he'd said something brief to her and gone immediately to his room. She'd sat on the floor in front of the tree and stared at it for a long time.

Now, watching their place two days before Christmas, I could see they had company. A couple and a pair of children: a matching set. Both kids had clean-cut, modish hairstyles, expensive looking jeans, and stylish, pop-culture t-shirts. I wondered if my childless pair were envious of their apparent familial bliss, especially when I saw the visiting woman turn and reveal an expectant curve.

They all settled in at the large dining room table. It seemed late, to me, for a supper, but I supposed that they were used to accommodating the late-evening demands of people in high positions. They sat close together, clasping hands and bowing heads. I could see my mark praying. I imagined the hypocritical words coming from his lips. In the years I could remember, I'd seen many genuine people of faith – people who were kind to one another, people who lived as if they actually believed in a higher power. But I'd seen too much of *this*. Inwardly ugly, violent, calloused people who used God as a justification for their own ambition or weak wills, or as a footnote in their cold and self-absorbed lives. As I watched them unlink their hands and pick up their shiny, silver-plated utensils, I thought primarily of two things. First, that his wife must loathe holding the hand that causes her so much pain and, secondly, that the silverware would look excellent on my table.

I settled in to watch them again, laying down and resting my cheek against the concrete ledge. They ate slowly. It was one of the few times men like these were obligated to slow down. I wondered again what they were talking about. Their faces were animated, eyes alight. The husband laughed, slapping the table with his too-large hand, and I saw his wife start. My eyes narrowed to slits.

I tried not to think about Lexi, but it was an impossible endeavor. The moisture in her eyes. The confusion in her tone. The taste of her mouth. The meaningless goodbye. Marcus had been right about women who trust too much; she had, indeed, told my secret. But he'd been wrong, too. It was she who ended up hurt.

I awoke with a start and realized I'd been sleeping. The orange glow in the sky told me dawn had come and gone. The bedroom light in the darkened apartment flickered on. I was trapped. There was no way I was going to risk a flight in the busy city during the day.

What now? I stood, slowly and cautiously, and walked around the inner sections of the roof. Nobody would be up here, especially in winter, in December. I could safely wait out the day. The stairwell structure provided shade and something solid to rest against. I settled in. I would wait until nightfall.

I watched my mark get ready for his day: tie his tie, comb his thinning hair. Had they opened some presents the night before, with the visiting family? Had they stayed up late into the night, talking or singing carols or doing whatever families do in the Christmas season? I was interested in seeing his wife during the day. I'd never really watched my marks during daylight hours. How would she fill her time?

I wondered how Lexi filled *her* daytime hours. She had graduated from high school already – early, she'd said. What had school been like for her? Had she been popular? Who were her friends? What classes were her favorites? Was she sad this morning when she woke up? Did she think about me?

I turned to focus again on the apartment in front of me. The husband was gone, and the wife was coming out of the shower in a long white towel. I watched her make her way into her bedroom. I wasn't voyeuristic, despite the nature of my work. My watching was professional: clean, calculated research. But I found myself watching this woman for no other reason than interest. She was, I guessed, in her mid-forties, although, aside from carefully disguised gray in her poker-straight hair, I could hardly tell. Shapely strong calves, smooth pale shoulders, and, if one ignored the bruises along her upper arms, flawless skin. Such a beautiful woman, and such a raw deal.

As the woman unwrapped the towel and stared at her body in her bedroom mirror, I quickly looked away. She should close her blinds. I stared down at my hands. I'd never used my hands to help anyone. But what could I do anyway? Flying was no super power. And, of course, I was supremely selfish. I deliberately looked at the suite below her apartment. There must be something there to distract me. No such luck. Aside from a white-lighted Christmas tree, the apartment was dark; its occupants were still sleeping, no doubt. I glanced back up and was mostly relieved to see her wearing gray yoga pants and sliding a fitted t-shirt over her head. She carefully tied an elastic around her hair in a high, young-style ponytail. She laced her runners, checked her reflection once, made a face, and left. I wished I were invisible, and I could venture to the edge of the roof and peer over. Instead, I leaned against the wall again and closed my eyes, wondering if I could sleep in the intense light. Again, the day was overrated.

Time passed, and sleep continued to elude me. I watched as the citizens of the daylight hours woke up and got ready for their waking lives. The routines were all different and yet painfully the same. The people were like cliché characters, written by a hack playwright: eager offspring, doting wives, loving husbands. Sham lives.

Movement in my mark's apartment caught my attention. She was back. She was on her cell phone, laughing. I realized that this was what a real smiled looked like on her face. She lay down on her bed, kicking off her shoes. Reaching over, she turned on her radio, still talking. She was a different person, without him. Didn't she see how her life would be if she hadn't tied herself to him? And why didn't she just leave? I watched her finish her conversation, look at the time on her cell phone, and then get up and go into the kitchen. She was starting supper. I imagined many of the people in areas like these had maids; in fact, I knew they did. Many of the women in these homes had, like the men, successful careers during which they worked long hours and came home exhausted. But not everyone had a maid, even when they could afford it.

I watched her remove defrosted meat from the fridge and then open her organized pantry and pull out cans and spices. She had no recipe, and she danced to something as she worked, relaxed and comfortable in her own home. Again, I was surprised by the contrast between this woman and the one I'd been watching for months. Supper in the oven, she began cleaning her bathroom: mopping the tiled floor, shining the mirror, wiping down the marbled counters. Her lips were moving; she was singing along to whatever it was she was listening to. When she went out again, I drifted in and out of sleep until she returned with several grocery bags and a new piece of artwork, a painting which she carefully hung up in the front hallway. She stood completely still and just stared at it for a moment, quiet. Then her shoulders sagged and she began to put away the groceries. The day was beginning to darken; soon I'd be able to leave my roofed prison and return to my home, such as it was. She was looking more agitated. She did and redid her hair, using the flat-iron on each section at least three time, then wetting it and trying again. She carefully applied her makeup; subtle eyeliner, muted red lipstick. She was readying herself for his return. He didn't deserve it.

Darkness descended. The table was set and candles lit when he walked through the door, glancing at her and greeting her briefly. He disappeared into his room and, like he did most evenings, removed his necktie, hanging it over the closet door, undid his top button, and rolled up his white sleeves. He returned to the dining room, where they sat together. It was Christmas Eve. Would they exchange presents this evening? Would they go to church? What did I care anyway? I needed to get off the roof, up into the air. Away from this family, this home, this repulsive display of domestic solitude. They were no less alone than I was. But she didn't need to be a prisoner. She chose it.

It was dark; people were beginning their Christmas traditions and celebrations. I would need to retire early this evening. Soon, little ones, all over the city, would be watching the sky, waiting for Santa Claus. I suspected I wouldn't make a very convincing substitute.

Back in my apartment, I tried to imagine what it would have looked like if I'd put up my own little Christmas tree. If I'd strung tiny colored lights, hung a star. Would it have made me feel better this Christmas Eve, when all I could feel was the ache of loneliness and the absence of Lexi? The image of the woman, sitting alone on the floor in front of her Christmas tree, abruptly came to mind, and I wished I could have seen the expression on her face. Had it brought her comfort, to have the symbol of peace and tradition in her loveless home? Suddenly glad for the stark honesty in my dreary one-room dwelling, I listened to the sound of police sirens from the street below and poured myself a bowl of cereal. Who cared about Christmas Eve, anyway?

I stayed in my apartment for the next six days; Christmas was a busy, unpredictable season, not to mention remarkably depressing these days. I had no desire to be out and about, so I hibernated. After a while, though, my own company annoyed me, and I realized I wasn't coping well with the boredom. I was sleeping too much; convoluted dreams of Lexi blended confusingly with images of the woman and fantasies of violent retribution against my mark. It was unlike me; it was time to simply finish the job and then move on. To get this city out of my veins.

Getting dressed, I remembered, this time, to pull on my black mask. I had gotten out of the practice of wearing it, but the fabric against my face felt comfortably familiar. I didn't plan to enter their place tonight but, if the opportunity arose, I'd take it. I put on the harness and wrapped the straps around my body. Glancing in the mirror once more, I thought how terrifying I must have looked when Lexi and I first met. Leaving through the window, I climbed onto the fire escape and then to the roof. From there, I was in the air, high above the city lights, breathing in the cool December air.

When I arrived across from their apartment and touched down, I wished I'd waited another night. I could hear, muted by the distance, the sound of his voice as he shouted at his wife. When I looked across, I almost winced as his red face contorted with the force of his words. She must have said something, because he grabbed her arms with both hands and shook her. Her head hit the wall and she reached out futilely to stop him. Finally, he pushed her, hard enough to send her across the room, out of his grasp, and into the end table. I could see the crystal vase shatter against the hardwood, scattering the flowers it held. She sat up quickly, holding her wrist, and scrambled backwards, through the glass to the wall.

What kind of man was I, to be calmly watching the scene before me? Like I had in dozens of other homes, between countless other couples just like them. This wasn't a new scene to me. *Never get involved. Focus on the job. Just the job.* I was no hero.

Still, I felt my pulse pounding as she held up her good arm to shield herself from the blows. It couldn't last forever; he would eventually wear himself out, as he always did. That or kill her.

I was relieved to see him shoving his arms through the sleeves of his leather coat. He was leaving. Good. She would survive this time. But what about the next? He slammed the door so hard that the painting she'd carefully hung in the entrance before Christmas fell from the wall and splintered as it hit the floor. She sat, her long hair hiding her face, her shoulders shuddering. I knew what I had to do. *Go home. Come back tomorrow. Or just forget about this whole thing. You don't really even need the money.* Instead, though, I stood on the ledge of the roof, clenching my fists.

And then I was in the air, and then on the balcony, and then entering the apartment. Her head flew up. She clambered to her feet and backed away.

I shook my head, putting my hand palm out towards her. "Listen. Just listen. Please, just listen, " Her eyes were wide, her mouth agape. "Listen, you need to leave him." My voice rang loud in my ears. "Let me take you away from here." She said nothing, taking a step back from me and shaking her head, hand over her mouth. "Listen! I'm not going to hurt you. I just – you need to get out." I was talking quickly, frantically. Was she listening? "I can take you away from here. Or – you can just pack up and leave. He'll kill you next time." Her eyes shifted to my wings now. She was quiet, staring. I lowered my voice. "You shouldn't be with someone like this. You just shouldn't. You don't need to stay. Let me help you." Still staring at my wings, she moved her head slightly. Was that a nod?

The front door swung open. He had come back, and I was standing in the doorway of his bedroom, masked and gloved, wings reflecting the points of light from the living room chandelier.

"What…?" A moment – it took a moment of stunned silence – and then, shouting, he charged toward me. I tried to move back, out of the way, but suddenly, he was on me, his hands around my throat, pinning my head hard against the floor. I could hear his wife screaming in the background, and I clawed at his shirt, at his face. The edges of the scene in front of me darkened; I breathed in frantically. Air. I groped blindly beside me, feeling a small, hard object – a shoe, maybe. Bringing it up hard and fast, I felt it connect with his skull, and he fell off. I clambered to my feet and, as he tried to get up, my fist connected solidly with his heavy jaw. My foot jabbed at his rib cage, and he rolled to escape my wild kicks.

He lunged towards me; I saw it too late, a glint of light from the sharp piece of crystal in his fist. Searing pain. I staggered backwards, and the man, breathing heavily, looked down at the blood-covered shard in his hand. I clutched at my side, feeling the sticky warmth soak through the fabric of my gloves. With an animal groan, I turned and limped to the balcony, pitching myself over the edge. I fell for a moment and then my wings instinctively lifted me, up past the apartment and into the sky. The world was a dizzying blur. I tried to push past the raw burning, focus on orienting myself. I needed to get back to my apartment and I needed to think in order to do it. My torso felt wet; I was losing too much blood, too quickly.

I pushed through the haze. I was closing in on my apartment. I could see the lighted window above my dark one. So close. I reached out to grab the fire-escape stairwell, to pull myself up. My fingers fumbled around the wrought-iron railing but, instead of finding my feet secure on the platform, I was grasping at the bars, falling, trying to catch the next one. My wings refused to respond and, seconds later, I was writhing on the snow, below the fire-escape, just next to the concrete street.

Shoes. White and brown shoes. I looked up, trying to breathe. The face wasn't really familiar but I felt like I should recognize him. Young, maybe my age or a little younger. The boy who'd been watching me from across the street.

9

"What's wrong with you?" So many potential replies occurred to me but, even if I'd wanted to answer him, I couldn't. My tongue refused to respond; a low moan is all I could manage. I reached out weakly to the stranger in front of me but pulled my hand back quickly to clutch my side again. His brow furrowed. "You're hurt." Again, a moan. I tried to nod. "Bad?" He leaned in close to try to see. I could tell he noticed the reddening of the snow beneath me now, and I could see him quickly make a decision. "I'll get you up to your place. You live on the third floor, right?" I attempted a movement I hoped resembled a nod. "Okay. You have to try to hold on to me. There's no way I can lift your dead weight." He was right. His collar bone protruded sharply from his neckline and his baggy jeans and oversized sweater didn't do much to hide his gaunt frame. He reached down and moved his arm under my shoulder. I tried my best to stand but my legs were weak. "Just hold on to me." The progress was slow and, somewhere in the back of my mind, it occurred to me I was out in the open; my wings were completely exposed. Any passerby would see. I tried to look behind me. "Nobody's around," he said, interpreting my anxious look correctly. "But we need to get inside."

We moved through the lobby and up the stairs. By this point, he was half dragging me, as if I had no muscles at all. Outside my suite he tried to lower me onto the floor, but he lost his grip and I fell, landing hard. I barely felt it. His fingers explored my pockets, searching for my keys. As soon as he found them, he flung open the door and, holding it open with one foot, dragged me unceremoniously through. Letting the door fall closed behind us, he grabbed my sweater off the couch. "Where're you hurt?" I moved my hands and saw his eyes widen. He handed me my sweater. "Hold this here." I did, and I could see his wheels working again. "Who can we call?" He looked at my wings. "Someone, Man. Anyone."

Lexi. I gestured for his phone. It felt like it took forever to dial ten simple digits; I knew her number, but I could barely think. It was ringing. I placed it in his outstretched palm.

"Hello?" He hesitated and then tried his best. "There's this guy – he's hurt – cut – says you know him." He glanced at me, listening. Then he lowered his voice to a whisper, as if that would make the information more believable. "He has wings." She must have responded immediately because he gave her my address and simple directions, telling her to hurry and bring any medical supplies that could help close a deep cut. And then he was there, offering me a drink, putting the couch cushion under my head, pushing the soaked sweater tight against my open wound. "I don't know what I'm doing, Man." I was feeling calmer now, starting to get cold. Would I die here, with this stranger? Would Lexi care? I'd left her the day before Christmas Eve and hadn't called her since. I heard a car stop outside, and the boy ran to the window to look outside. "It's a cab – a redhead." He ran to the door, and soon they came back together.

"What happened?" Her voice was breathy, high-pitched. She glanced down at me and her face lost its color. "Joshua. What happened?"

I smiled weakly at her – or I meant for it to be a smile, anyway.

"I don't know," the boy said, "but he's bleeding and we need to do something about it."

"We need to call an ambulance."

"We can't." She looked up at him, frowning, and he repeated, more slowly, "You must know we can't."

"Okay." Her voice was shaking, but I saw her deliberately calm herself; she straightened her shoulders. "Okay." Steady now. She was all business. "I brought my Dad's work bag, from the clinic. It has a bunch of supplies in it – and antibiotics." She took the towel away, carefully, making sure it hadn't dried to the wound yet. Her eyes welled; I saw her waver. "We need to get all this stuff off. His shirt, these stupid harnesses." They half rolled me on my side, and I tried to stifle a groan. I heard fabric tearing, and then I felt her pulling at my wings. "Get these things off. I need to see what I'm doing."

"What are you talking about?"

"The wings. They're mechanical."

The guy's voice sounded strained. "He told you they're mechanical?"

"Yeah. Remote control. Attached with the harnesses –" I felt the rush of air as she yanked the straps free, and I heard her suck in her breath. I knew she was seeing the truth; four, clear, insect-like wings protruding from between my shoulder blades. I felt the warm tips of her fingers explore the joining between the wings and my skin. I was losing vision. "What on…" The voices came from far away. And then, my world was mercifully black.

The first thing I noticed was the searing pain in my side, and the next was that I was, indeed, alive. I was lying on the floor on my back, the weight of my body heavy against the wings stretched out beneath me. Their voices were close by: quiet, indistinguishable words, spoken at a whisper and blending together. Burning thirst.

"Could I –" My voice was hoarse, and Lexi came to my bedside immediately, putting a cup of water in my hand. "Thanks." I drank. She sat beside me, running her hand along my hairline. Her fingers were cool on my forehead.

"Hey, Dragonfly," she said softly. She didn't hate me. "I didn't know if you would pull through." I waited for her to ask me again what happened but she didn't. She sat in silence and looked down at me. Her eyes, though, held a thousand questions. I wondered what she wanted to ask first. *What was I? Where did I come from? Who was I, really?* For the first time in my life, I owed somebody an explanation.

"I'm Eric, by the way." A muffled voice called from the table. His mouth was full.

"Joshua," I offered weakly.

"So I hear. So, what's your deal?" Lexi shot him a quick warning look, and he answered with a long, drawn-out sigh and loud chewing.

"Shhh," Lexi whispered to me, softly. "You should try to rest. I tried to clean your injury, but I don't know how good a job I did. I'd never done anything like that before, and I'm worried about infection. We were just really lucky he stabbed you where he did – I couldn't have done anything if he'd hit any organs. But still, you have to be careful. I stopped the bleeding and stitched everything up the best I could – but even with it stitched up like this, it'll be pretty easy to open."

"You shoulda seen her work," Eric offered from across the room. "Stitched you up like a pro. I thought I was gonna be sick with all that blood. She didn't even flinch."

I squeezed her hand. "I believe it."

"Don't be so sure." She smiled gently down at me. "You're gonna have a pretty wicked looking scar later. Apparently, stitching someone up is a lot harder than it looks when my Dad does it on an animal."

"Plus I bet you've never seen him work on a bug." Eric's voice held laughter, but her lips pursed into a hard line.

"Ignore him," Lexi said. She shifted her eyes to the wings underneath me. "I can't believe they're real." Her hands were clasped in her lap now. As if she couldn't help herself, she asked, "Can I touch them?"

"Sure." Nobody had ever touched my wings; aside from when she had been blindly trying to remove them from my body, I'd never even known what touch would feel like, and I had been so out of my mind with pain then that I had hardly even noticed. Now, though, as she ran her fingers along the edges of my top right wing and then flattened her palm against it gently, I closed my eyes and concentrated on the warm sensation. "I don't know how to thank you, Lexi. For saving my life."

"Truth would be nice." Not angry. Just matter-of-fact. "But not right now. Rest now." It wasn't difficult for me to do what she asked. I was tired. Hazy. Something had been in the water she'd given me. Something was making the pain ebb and my head feel fuzzy and good. Calm. Seeing me glance at the water, she explained, "Fentanyl and antibiotics. They'll help you sleep and get better faster."

"Thanks," I mumbled, and the light vanished again.

When I awoke, the lights in the apartment were out and the curtains were drawn. The streetlights outside gleamed through the thin fabric, illuminating the two figures slumped together on the couch. Eric slept, his head resting on the armrest. Lexi's body rested on his, her head on his bony chest. I felt a flash of something I didn't quite recognize and definitely didn't like. I struggled to get up, throwing the thick blanket off my body, feeling cool air brush over my naked chest. Pain, but less than I remembered. Lexi stirred and sat up. "You're awake."

"How long have I been out?"

"Off and on for a week now. You had a pretty bad fever."

"A week. Your folks worried?"

"No. I told them I went skiing at a friend's cottage."

I sat quietly beside her. "Sorry I dropped off the face of the earth after Christmas."

"It wasn't the first time, anyway. And that's all your sorry for?"

"No. Guess I'm least sorry for that. The disappearing act: that was my attempt at doing the right thing. You know now, right, that life with me could never be normal?"

"I don't want normal."

"You do. You don't realize it, but you do. Ordinary is much better than – whatever I am. Whatever our life would be."

I'd said our life. She was silent for a moment and then asked, "Why didn't you tell me they were real? At least, eventually. After we knew each other? Why did you keep lying to me?"

"I don't know. I never tell anyone they're real. That's why I wear the harnesses."

"But even after you got to know me?"

"I guess," I went for honesty, "I never really thought that this…" I gestured to the two of us, "could ever be anything permanent."

"Thanks." She was silent.

Finally, I touched her hand. "You think I didn't want it to be? Every time I left your place, I felt sick. But I don't get to have a regular life. And I don't get to have you. That's just the way it has to be for me."

She shook her head, started to say something, but then changed her mind and fell silent. "We'll see." She squeezed my hand now. After a moment of quiet, she asked, "So, what are you, anyway?"

"What am I?"

"Did someone make you – like that? Or were you born that way?"

I shrugged. "I honestly don't know. I remember almost nothing from when I was really young. I don't really remember my parents. I just – this is me. This is who I am. I can't give you any more than that."

"How many people know about you?"

"I have a contact in each city I've been to – and I've been all over the world."

"All over the world!" I knew she'd like that. "What do you mean, a contact?"

"People who help me find places to live. Get me my groceries. Point me in the direction of the best area to hit."

"Ah. And you trust them?"

"More or less. But I pick people…" I tried to find a way to tactfully explain my selection process. "… who aren't so well off in life. Who would be grateful for a little money and friendship, rather than for the fame offered by exposing me. And who wouldn't be believed anyway, if they told."

"Who else?"

"There used to be Nik. He was the guy who taught me what I needed to know to survive."

"Nik. Your guardian angel."

"Hardly. Maybe at first." His image came to my mind again: gruff, unsmiling, merciless.

"What ever happened to him?

"He and I…" I paused. "We had a fundamental disagreement on ways of doing business." That was one way to put it. "Every now and then, when I'm in the area, I'll circle around our old place. But I never go back. And he's long gone, anyway."

"What was he like?"

"He just – he was practical. He didn't let people get in his way." Nik's particular brand of skills would have come in handy in my latest altercation though. I wouldn't have almost died. And there would definitely have been no witnesses. "Anyway, besides Nik, there's you. And Eric, now, I guess."

"That's it?"

"Yep." I hesitated. "Well, and the guy who did this," I gestured to the white gauze taped to my side, "and his wife."

She looked down at it, touching the clear binding. "Has that ever happened before – on the job?"

I shook my head.

Eric shifted beside her, stretching now and sitting up. "Hey, you're awake." He leaned out past Lexi to look at me. "Welcome back."

"Thanks."

He stood and sauntered across the room. He opened the curtain to let some light in, and then he began rummaging through my cooler.

A thought occurred to me. "So, did I make the news?"

He and Lexi exchanged a long look. He grabbed a folded paper from the table and tossed it over to me, just before taking an apple from the cooler. He leaned against the peeling paint of the bare walls and chewed loudly, watching me as I opened the paper.

"It makes you sound very strong, if that makes you feel any better," Lexi said softly.

"Wonderful. And look, front page." I knew at a glance it was about me. "Winged thief terrorizes couple," I read aloud, in my best impression of a news anchor from the nineteen fifties. Nobody laughed. I scanned the rest of the article quickly. *Broken window, viciously attacked.* An embellishment, at best. *Some kind of a winged device.* "This is good news," I told them. "Nobody knows they're real." I also noticed the article mentioned that his estranged wife had no comment. Estranged.

"Not the point," Lexi said. Eric was silent. "People know what you're doing. It mentions a string of high-rise robberies throughout the country. People will be looking for you."

"They won't find me."

"They'll also be expecting you."

"I'll manage. I'll go somewhere else."

"Just like that."

"Yeah. It's what I do. I'll move on."

She was quiet for a moment, then wordlessly got up, shoved on her boots, and left. I didn't try to stop her. I wasn't completely dense. I was planning to leave, likely for good, and I'd made no offer to take her with me. I looked up at Eric. He shrugged. "What can you do, Man?" As if the opportunist wasn't gloating secretly.

"I can't take her with me."

"Guess not." He shifted. "But where do you think you're going to be able to go where they won't be looking for you? You know, if you made headlines here, it could be picked up by the global press. Especially in developed places. Places with money." He leaned back again, a little too casually, as the words sunk in. I hadn't thought of that. Not that I was looking forward to getting back to work. "But you know, I could help you out."

I looked at him sharply. "Why would you do that?"

He returned my gaze evenly. "I don't know. Have no job – no prospects. It would get me out of town, give me something to do. And what can I say? I'm a nice guy."

He was lying now. We both knew it, but I couldn't seem to turn him down. "What do you have in mind?"

"Don't know." Another obvious lie. "But we could figure it out as we go. You know you can't stay here."

"Sure." I forced a casual tone. "Sounds like a plan to me."

"What sounds like a plan?" I hadn't even heard her enter.

"That was quick."

"I didn't go anywhere. I got to the front door and realized I was being a child." I nodded, about to agree, when she added, "You're scared. I get that. But I don't intend on letting you let me go again. Now, what's a good idea?"

Eric cleared his throat. "I offered to help your friend out while he figures out what to do next. There's this abandoned place I know, in Colorado. We can crash there for a bit while things cool off."

"Yeah." I was game. "Eric will give me directions and I'll fly out there. He'll drive and we'll meet up."

"Actually, Eric *and* I will meet up with you." She met my eyes.

Eric raised his eyebrows and grinned at me. "Really?"

"Lexi, it's not a good idea. We don't know exactly where we're going." I looked back at Eric's stupid face. "And I don't know anything about this guy. I'm not comfortable with you alone in a car with him, going who-knows-where."

"Well, I'm not comfortable with being left alone again," she shot back. "I'm not comfortable with you going who-knows-where with him either."

"Thanks," Eric chimed in.

Ignoring him, she finished triumphantly, "And I'm not comfortable with you thinking you get to tell me what to do. I'm coming, okay?"

"It's fine with this guy," Eric said, pointing at himself, daring me to counter her again.

"Not okay."

She crossed her arms over her chest. "Well, you're outvoted."

I sighed. I should forget the whole thing, leave now, and figure out where to go on my own. But the thought of leaving her with Eric made me sick. Besides, I was convinced, quite irrationally, that I needed to know what it was he was doing. No matter what it cost me. "Fine. But I'm not flying then." As way of gracious explanation, I added, "I don't want to risk missing our meeting spot."

"So you're coming in the vehicle?" Lexi asked. They both simultaneously glanced at my wings.

"They're flexible."

Lexi smothered a smirk and Eric furrowed his brow. "Are you sure that's a good idea? It's, like, a 27 hour drive – and that's if we don't stop."

"Positive." Not at all.

"Fine." We had a plan. All that was left were the details.

10

We didn't have much time to prepare. Now that I was all over the news, to any joker who half-remembered seeing me frequenting my apartment, what had before seemed like a trick of the light or imagination, would suddenly seem plausible. Now that I was in the public mind, I existed.

It didn't take me long to figure out, though, that Eric didn't need much time to prepare anyway. He was simply miming the actions of someone figuring things out. He knew exactly what he was doing. As we readied to leave, I imagined ways to make Lexi stay behind. I could tell her I didn't care about her at all or that I found her annoying, unattractive, stifling. That would be fair thing to do. Get her out of my life, permanently. But I couldn't make myself do it. I had a feeling she wouldn't believe me anyway, if I had. She was stubbornly glued to me.

She did, at one point during our two days of preparation, return home to get a bag of her things and to say goodbye to her family. She slipped out in the morning while I slept. Lexi told me later that her father had cried when she told him she was planning to go on a road trip with one of her friends. She said it was because he was disappointed in her, but I was pretty sure he would simply miss her. Her mother, she said, had tried to keep her composure but had slipped her a wad of her own personal spending money, and her brother had solemnly made her promise to bring back souvenirs.

Eric pretended to go about figuring out the mundane details: what route we would take, how much gas we would need, where exactly we could stay. He programmed our course into Lexi's GPS and, when it spit out the expected time, he acted as if it were new information. Lexi was convinced by his performance and believed him when he explained again about the abandoned cabin he knew about, in the rural west, where we could go to figure out our next move. It was secluded, he said, and completely safe. I believed half of his statement.

The day of our departure, as we waited in the darkening apartment for night to fall and provide us our opportunity, Eric slept on the couch, leaving Lexi and me to finish packing the cooler with the groceries he'd bought with Lexi's money. He hadn't yet asked me any questions, which, of course, made me trust him even less. Lexi was full of questions. *Could I remember what my mother looked like, at least a little? How did I decide I could trust Nik? How did I learn to do what I did? What was my first flying experience like?*

The flying question was an easy one. I couldn't say for sure if it were my first flying experience, but I felt it could have been. The strangeness of it had struck me at the time. Nik and I had been in the field outside the rundown, abandoned barn we'd been living in. He'd fixed it up, made it liveable, and it had been home for a while. We were standing in the field, several months after he'd found me.

"Try them out," he'd said. Not a question. I'd been afraid. Could I even control them? But I never questioned Nik. And he'd said that I would never learn what I was capable of if I didn't learn to trust my instincts. And so I did. I took a breath, stretched out my wings, and they did the rest.

I tried to explain to Lexi how it had felt, feeling them suddenly come to life, as if they'd been waiting for the opportunity, hearing the sound of them beating furiously in the air for the first time, experiencing the sensation of rising effortlessly into the sky, weightless. I was up high above the roof of the barn and Nik was nothing but a speck. The world below me had disappeared and I was simply flying. Powerful and strong and fearless.

If Nik had called after me or worried about me at all, I never knew it. "All other flying experiences have paled in comparison to that first taste of freedom. Until I met you," I told her. I liked the thought that she'd been able to be part of that world, even for those brief moments in time.

When evening came, we were ready. We had finished packing, checked and re-checked our route, and counted Lexi's cash. Just before ten, we crept down the stairs to Eric's waiting, rusted-out, red four-passenger car. I wondered again why I was going through with this. Of course, I had nothing worth losing anyway. Except Lexi, and I never really had her in the first place.

Eric drove and Lexi sat in the passenger seat beside him. There was no room in the back with me anyway, with my wingspan and necessarily awkward sprawl. I sat in the center of the bench seat, my four wings stretched across the car, filling the space beside me and following the curves of the side window. Anyone looking inside would think we had hung translucent, shimmering curtains – strange, of course, but not nearly as strange as the truth. Eric adjusted the rear view mirror to look at me. "Ready?" he asked.

"Of course." I gritted my teeth as he repeated his question to Lexi.

"As I'll ever be," she said. The car sputtered to life, and he pulled away from the curb.

The city looked different from street level. Congested. Dull, even. As we waited for the light to turn green, I watched an ordinary couple pass by, hands clasped, laughing about something.

People were the same everywhere.

That first night's journey was more arduous than it should have been. Adjusting to the rolling motion of the vehicle was not as easy as I'd assumed, and it didn't help that Eric's stereo didn't work. My wound had been healing better than we'd expected and the absorbable stitches had already started to disappear, so the last thing I wanted to do was reopen it. Even outside the city, surrounded by open space, sleep alluded me. Of course, I didn't generally sleep at night anyway, so it didn't surprise me that I spent the first leg of our journey wide-awake. And with the noise of the highway and the wind, it was impossible to hear anything beyond brief snatches of the conversation in the front seat. Their attempts to make small talk with me, therefore, were wasted. Not that I was sure I could say anything intelligible anyway. Riding in a vehicle produced a very different sensation than flying did. They entertained one another by what seemed to be light banter and maybe less than riveting conversation. What did I care, anyway?

I wondered if whatever Eric was scheming was dangerous. Was this a trap? Maybe, like Marcus always feared about every person he met, Eric intended to hand me over to the government for secret testing. I looked at the back of Eric's head, his shaggy brown hair pressed comfortably against the torn, faded bucket seats. It was unlikely he'd be working for anyone in power. He was undoubtedly planning something though. After some time, as the sunrise began to light the sky, Eric shifted in his seat. "Hey, Man, you hungry?"

"Getting there." Or at least, I should be. I couldn't tell, with the rolling motion of the car making me lightheaded and turning my stomach to an ocean.

"There's a place up here where we could stop. Lexi and I could bring you something."

I made a sound that I hoped meant I was agreeable.

"Eric says it's a diner," Lexi said. "Want something specific or should I surprise you?"

"Surprise me." I tried not to grimace. As they walked towards the small, off-white diner, I slouched in the back seat and tried not to picture them sharing a plate of hash browns, laughing at some private joke.

When they came out ten minutes later, I'd managed to work myself up into a fairly unfriendly mood, but seeing them return so quickly took the edge from my voice. "Thanks, Lexi," I told her genuinely as she handed me a breakfast sandwich and slid into her side. Eric slammed his door.

"You're welcome," she answered, opening the paper wrapping on hers. "We thought it would be quicker to take it to go. Plus, I didn't want you to get cold out here."

"I told her I'd left you the keys," Eric said. "You could have started the car and let it run."

"Waste of gas," she shot back. I heard him sigh heavily as the car sputtered to life. "So," she asked me over the cough of the engine, "how's your trip been so far?"

"Amazing," I replied dryly, and she laughed, catching my meaning.

"I can imagine."

"And what about you? What have you been chatting about up there?"

"Nothing *amazing.* Just keeping each other awake. Talking about school and stuff."

"Do you miss it?"

"Not really. And I guess I'll go back again someday, to college or something…" She trailed off, not sure how she would finish that sentence. She attempted weakly, "When I figure out what I want to be."

I didn't miss a beat. "Obviously a doctor."

"Yeah, I wouldn't be so sure if I were you. Those stitches aren't gonna be pretty."

"Don't you know? Chicks dig scars. And besides, you saved my life."

"You're welcome." She flipped around in her seat again, as the car continued flying down the highway. I was still sick from the drive. There was no way I could eat this, no matter how nice the sentiment. I reached past my large wing to roll down the window and let the wind take my sandwich. The air funnelled past, filling the car with a cool breeze. Eric closed window and I heard him click the child lock. *No fresh air for me.*

I watched the sun on the horizon. We had to have been on the road for a good eight hours, maybe more. I didn't ask about the time though. The thought of another twenty hours cooped up in here was almost unbearable – to have an exact number seemed worse somehow. I leaned back and closed my eyes. Maybe I could sleep. Normally, I'd have been in hours ago and sound asleep by now. If I could just shut out the motion and the highway, I'd be able to relax. A thumping from beneath the car assured me that sleep wasn't going to be a luxury I'd get to enjoy anytime soon.

"What's that?" Lexi asked, as Eric pulled the car to the shoulder.

Eric sighed. "Sounds like a flat." I wished I could see his face. Was this another trick? An opportunity to stop and meet up with someone?

"Do you have a spare?" I asked.

He turned to face me. His forehead creased in a deep frown. "You think I'm an idiot?" Debatable. "Of course I have a spare. I just… it's just annoying." The flat was clearly unplanned. But he didn't like the delay, which affirmed what I already knew. Somebody was expecting us.

"I'd offer to help…" I said.

He rolled his eyes. "Right." He opened his door. "It's fine."

"I could help," Lexi offered, but he was shaking his head before she finished.

"Ever changed a tire?"

"No."

"Then you'll slow me down. No offense."

"None taken," she said.

"I'll be quick," he said, slamming the door. I settled myself, trying to get as comfortable as I could as I waited.

I heard her shift in her seat. "So, seriously, how's the drive been for you so far? You didn't give me a real answer before."

"Uncomfortable."

"Bet you wish you were flying."

"Sure. But makes more sense for me to be here for now." I wished I could see past my wings, stretching over the glass of the windows.

"Because you don't know where we're headed?"

"Because I can keep an eye on that guy."

She laughed. The sound was almost musical in the small vehicle. "Eric's harmless." She turned in her seat to look at me. "And he saved your life, Joshua." The car jerked as Eric jacked it up.

"You saved my life." I corrected her. She raised her eyebrows. I shrugged. "But I guess Eric helped."

"Right. You really still don't trust him, hey?"

"I don't."

"Then why did you come?" It was a fair question. I wasn't quite sure I knew the answer.

"I made the front page. Eric's offer to help me lay low seemed… intriguing. And I didn't see many other options." We both knew it wasn't true, at least the part about the options. There were always choices. Maybe less than ideal ones, but surely better than traveling across the country with someone I didn't trust – and wasn't fond of on a personal level either. "And anyway," I added slowly, "I had nowhere else I needed to be."

"Fine," she said. "Why else?"

I stared at her for a moment. "Maybe I wanted to know what he was up to," I finally admitted. "He clearly knows where we're going. He has some kind of plan. I want to know what it is."

"Why don't you just ask him?"

"Right. Like he's going to suddenly feel the need for honesty. This seems like the most direct way to get the truth. I just wish you hadn't insisted on coming."

She blinked. "Wow. Thanks." She turned around abruptly, settling back into her seat.

"I didn't mean it like that. Lexi, you know I didn't. It's not that I don't want you here. It's just that I don't know where we're going. And I don't trust him. I shouldn't have let you come, because what if I can't protect you?"

She laughed again, but this time there was no music in the tone. "First of all, you don't get to decide where I go. Eric's running this trip, and he said I could come. So here I am. Second of all, I didn't ask you to protect me. And I don't need you to. You say you don't trust *him*? All you do is lie to me. Don't forget how we met."

"I don't." I reached forward and touched her shoulder. She was right, of course. I was a liar and a thief. Or I had been. Now, I didn't know anything anymore. "It changed my life." The words were out before I knew I was going to say them. "*You* changed my life."

She tilted her head, resting her ear against my fingers. The car jolted as it moved back down. We were out of alone time. It was probably a good thing. I didn't need any more time to admit to things I had no right to feel in the first place.

11

"Miss me?" Eric said with a grin as he swung his lanky frame back into the car.

"Desperately." She cleared her throat and then smiled lightly at him. "Can I drive the next stretch?"

"Sure. I'll show you how she drives best," Eric said. They switched spots and Lexi turned the key. I leaned back. Already, the noise of the car was drowning out their words, but I could see Eric explaining to her how to grasp the gearshift and demonstrating the precise technique needed to pop the clutch. They were laughing. Her brow was furrowed, but she looked relaxed, happy. This was how things should be for her. Not with Eric, of course, but with somebody. She deserved to be happy.

I fought the new motion sickness as she worked to figure out how the gearshift worked, but she eventually got the hang of it. We drove for what felt like an eternity before we turned down a stretch of gravel road and drove a few miles off the main highway. "We've been on the road for twelve hours. Just under halfway there. I'm thinking you need to stretch your legs," Lexi called back to me, "or your wings or something."

"Lexi…" Eric said, touching her hand.

"That would be great," I interrupted him. She was right. I was aching to get out of the car. The fact that Eric didn't want us to stop only intensified the need. Finally, she pulled to a stop and I practically fell out of the car. Solid ground had never felt so beautiful.

I sensed my wings anxious to be in the air. I barely managed to glance around to ensure there were no onlookers before I let them carry me up. The pressure of the wind and the open sky seemed to bring me back to life. Twelve hours in a tiny space like that was too much. "Joshua!" Eric called faintly from below. I knew I would be little more than a spec by now. I was pretty sure he wished I were tethered to his wrist. I was tempted to just keep flying – over the fields, away from Eric with his scheme and Lexi with her inexplicable hold on me.

The sky was so different out here, not only because it was daylight, but because there were no buildings or artificially bright lights. Only sky above and earth below. "Joshua!" Eric's barely discernible voice beckoned again. I could keep going, but then I'd never know what he wanted with me. And I'd never know that Lexi was safe.

I forced myself back down and, wordlessly, I got into the car. Lexi looked hurt, and I suspected she'd wanted me to offer to take her up. I hadn't even thought of it. Eric would have been watching us. I wasn't sure why, but it seemed like it should be something private, something between Lexi and me. Eric took the wheel. As we started our drive, I closed my eyes. It was still morning, but that made it my nighttime, and I was tired of feeling, anyway.

I drifted in and out of consciousness for the next leg of our journey. At one point, they stopped for food but, through my fog of sleep, I declined their offer to bring me some. The road didn't agree with me. When I finally woke, it was pitch black, aside from our headlights shining down the highway before us. I could hear a quiet, steady breathing and, through the rear-view mirror, I could see Lexi at the wheel and Eric, his head on the passenger side window, sleeping beside her. My movement in the back must have caught her eye because she subtly shifted her gaze and looked at me in the mirror. "Good morning, so to speak."

"Good morning." I leaned forward, raising my voice over the sound of the highway.

"Sleep well?"

"Not particularly."

"Could have fooled me. You were snoring pretty hard back there."

"Boredom," I insisted.

"How's your injury?"

"Good. Can barely feel it now."

"Mm." She looked in her rear view mirror again at me. "That's good. Here, eat something." She handed back a wrapped sandwich. This time, I ate it. "It's a good sign," she said. "It means you're feeling better." She was right. I was getting used to the motion of the car and the sound of the highway, although I was still a long way from liking it.

"So, how long until we're there?" I looked at the dark road in front of her. "We must be getting pretty close."

"A few hours. It's just after ten. Eric and I are taking turns now." I saw her stifle a yawn.

"So, how'd you get stuck on the night shift?"

"Volunteered, of course."

"Why's that?"

She looked at me through the mirror again. "Why do you think?"

I shifted and changed the subject abruptly. "Do you think Eric would mind if we pulled over for a few minutes again?"

"He's not the one driving, is he? Where should I get off?"

I scanned the darkness. My eyes, of course, functioned much better than hers in the dark, and I could see a great deal farther.

"You could turn down one of these side roads, if you want. Or you could just pull over along here. There's hardly any traffic."

After a moment of indecision, she pulled the car over. I hesitated. Then, I heard myself saying, "Listen. I don't have a harness with me. But if you trust me, and you're up for it, I can take you for a quick flight. You know… if you want." Apparently, I hadn't regained my sanity. In the middle of nowhere, on a main highway, with no safety precautions. At least it wasn't daylight. I was instantly rewarded with one of her childlike grins.

"Of course." No doubt. We quietly got out of the vehicle. I could imagine Eric's face if he woke up while we were gone and the scenarios that would run through his head. I hoped that he *would* wake up and that he'd think we'd flown off together.

Instead, our flight was short. I tried to commit the moment to memory, to take a mental snapshot of the way her arms felt snugged around my waist, clutching the back of my shirt in her fists as if her life depended on it, my arms supporting her weight entirely, and the night sky enveloping us as if we were the only two people in existence. If nothing good ever happened again, I hoped I could remember the way this moment felt, with her body, tight against mine in the cool night air. I knew it would be enough to carry me through.

Too soon, we were back in the car, back on the road, making our way west. Eric was still asleep, and Lexi's light chatter made the ride bearable. After a few hours, he woke up, and they switched spots. As Eric got back into the driver's side, he shot a quick glance my way. "Good to see you're still here. I dreamed you'd up and flown away."

I forced civility into my voice. "Wouldn't dream of leaving." Eric and I both knew that Eric was planning something and lying about his intentions. But he was, at the same time, being entirely himself. He was also obviously enamored with Lexi. I couldn't blame him for that.

Soon, Lexi's breathing deepened, a rhythmic hum filling the car. I smiled into the darkness. Finally, she slept.

"She's kinda something, hey?" Eric asked. I wasn't sure if he were actually talking to me or simply thinking aloud, so I didn't answer. "Do you see yourselves together?"

I realized he was addressing me. "What do you mean, together?" I asked, although I was pretty sure I knew.

"You know, happily ever after."

"No. I see her going back home to her family."

"Without you?"

I didn't hesitate. "Without me."

There was another beat of silence. "Mind if I take a shot?"

"You can try. But I don't think you'll have any luck."

He snorted. "No? Why not?" When I didn't reply, he laughed. "You like her."

"Of course."

"But you don't want to be with her?"

"I'm not right for her. You aren't either." Whether he wanted to face it or not, it was true. "You're not stable. You don't have a good job, with a high-rise somewhere. You can't take care of her. Think about it. I don't know what your game is here, but I know it's not one that can give Lexi the lifestyle she's used to."

"And you think that would make her happy?" he asked. I pushed the image of the man who'd stabbed me with the broken vase from my mind. "I don't know her that well but, from what I can see, she doesn't seem to care about money and definitely not about stability".

"Maybe not now. But that kind of thing will matter to her later on. When she's trying to make a life for herself."

"And what makes you an expert on all things Lexi?"

"I've seen enough of rich people to know that they tend to value their money. And whether she sees it now or not, she's one of them. It's the kind of life she deserves."

He shrugged. "It's the kind of life we all deserve. Or nobody does." I didn't reply. I thought of the stack of cash I had in the bottom of my bag. It would last me a long time, but not forever. It certainly wasn't enough to provide anyone with any kind of stable life. Besides, even if I'd had all the money in the world, stability wasn't in my cards.

"Listen, Eric. A girl like Lexi is inherently better than you or I," I said. His fingers tightened on the wheel. He didn't want to hear it, but I could tell he knew it was true. "She just is. There's something special about her. Besides the contacts and the amazing hair."

"Her hair *is* amazing."

"Uh-huh. But beyond that. She has something special."

"From the guy who has wings! Man, if I could fly…"

"If you could fly, you'd be stuck hiding. Stuck alone."

"You have Lexi," he said quietly.

"Not really. And not forever. Everything is temporary."

"Everything is temporary for everyone. At least you can fly."

Lexi shifted slightly, and we both fell silent. As we flew down the highway, I tried not to think about Eric's intentions. It would be convenient for him if I were gone. But he didn't seem evil-intentioned, despite the covert plans he was enacting. I wondered if he had family somewhere – people who loved him and cared whether or not he were okay. I thought again of Nik. Everything about my education had been serious and thorough: read, work, study. Most of it, of course, had been focused on how to steal from the regular rich but the other stuff – the math, the science, the literature – had been there too. Beyond education, though, Nik and I never had a relationship. There were no stories read to me by my bedside, no asking me about my day, no indication that he cared about me beyond how well I was learning whatever it was he was trying to teach me. I wondered if it would have made a difference, had he spent time showing me any sort of affection. Instead, I'd always gotten the vague impression that he disliked me. I had spent my time, early on at least, trying to earn his approval. I had failed.

I looked at Eric, hands still white-knuckled on the wheel, and wondered if he'd ever worried about his parents' approval. The three of us were so different; we were all together and yet all completely alone.

I knew we were nearing our destination when Eric started slowing down as we passed highway markers, reading carefully as he went. It was pitch black aside from the headlights. "We're getting close now?" I stated the obvious as a question.

"Yeah, the property is right around here somewhere." We turned off the main highway and drove in silence for a long while. I could tell he knew exactly where we were going now because he sped up a little, merely scanning for the correct place to turn off. I glanced at Lexi, worried. If he had some sinister purpose, I would have to protect her.

Why had I allowed her to come in the first place? Was I really so selfish that I would endanger Lexi, simply for the fleeting pleasure of her company? I had known Eric was up to something and I had brought her anyway. He slowed. As he turned down an unmarked gravel road, I looked for a clue as to where we were going. Far ahead of us was a structure, shrouded partially by trees. I suspected that was our destination.

"Is that the place?" I asked. He started slightly.

"You can see it from here?"

"Good eyesight."

"Yeah, that's the place." He slowed again as we approached and pulled into the rough-hewn driveway.

"This place is – abandoned?" Lexi asked. It seemed to be dawning on her that there were details he must have taken care of in advance, before we'd even talked about setting out together. "When – how did you find it? How did you know it would be abandoned?"

"I have contacts," he said. He was looking closely at me now, in the mirror. I could guess he was trying to decide whether or not I would see this thing through. As we coasted to a stop, I could see there was a light on in the living room of the small farmhouse. The curtains were drawn but a sliver of white alerted me to the fact that there was likely someone inside. I never should have allowed Lexi to come. I had no idea what we would be walking into.

Eric swung his lanky frame out of his seat and, as Lexi and I followed him to the rear of the car, I grabbed her arm, slowing her. He pulled his bag out and started towards the house but, as we reached the trunk, I leaned in close to Lexi.

"When I head towards Eric, lock yourself in the car." She didn't need to hear anything else. She nodded quickly, and I grabbed my bag and caught up with Eric, who was lingering between the house and the vehicle, watching me uncertainly. I swung my arm around him in an unexpected gesture of false camaraderie. "Well, Partner, let's go." The car door slammed, and Eric glanced behind us. "She's going to wait in the car," I said. He'd left the keys in the ignition and I was glad to know she could at least attempt an escape, should something happen. I wondered how long she would wait out there for me. "After you."

Eric glanced sharply at me. "You think I would let anything happen to her?"

"I don't know anything about you, other than you haven't asked me anything about who I am or where I'm from, and I would bet my life on the fact that you didn't need a GPS to tell you where we were going."

"If you knew so much," Eric said, flinging open the front door, "why did you bring her? I'm not the bad guy. I don't have some evil plot up my sleeve. I'm just doing what I was told." He gestured to the interior of the room now, and I followed his gaze.

"Hello, Joshua," Nik greeted me casually, leaning against the brick of the unlit fireplace. "Glad you could make it."

12

I said nothing to the man before me now. The vitality I remembered so clearly in him was gone; his cheeks were sunken, skin ashen, eyes hollow. Like a walking death. “Sorry for all the secrecy,” Nik said. “I was afraid you wouldn’t come and it was imperative that I see you.”

“I would have come.”

He shrugged. “I couldn’t risk that you wouldn’t. I told Eric to get you by any means.”

“Good for you. Why?”

“I needed to tell you some things, before it’s too late.”

“You’re dying.” It wasn’t a question but he nodded.

“I am. We all are, actually, but I’m on my way out right now.”

“What’s wrong with you?”

“I don’t know. But I’m not getting any better.”

Eric cleared his throat. “Can I bring Lexi in now?” he asked.

Nik raised his eyebrows. “Lexi?”

“A friend. She knows,” I said.

“Not good.”

I knew how Nik believed we should deal with problems. He tended to think permanent solutions were always the most effective. It was the primary reason we'd parted company. "This guy knows, " I said.

"He works for me," Nik said. "He knows he'll be well paid, if he does what he's told. And what will happen if he doesn't. Fear and money make excellent companions."

"She actually *care*s about me."

"So much less binding, when the affection starts to wane."

Eric shifted and coughed slightly. "She's out there waiting. She saved his life, you know, Nik."

"She did? You're a lucky man, Joshua. I just wish –" he turned his gaze to Eric again, "that you'd let me know you were bringing her. But you might as well invite her in now." I didn't like the way he said it, but I couldn't very well leave her in the car forever. And he knew about her now, anyway. As Eric disappeared, Nik said, "We have much to talk about, Joshua. But not right now."

Lexi came in, looking hesitant, and I reached out my hand to her. She took it quickly. "Lexi. Good to meet you." His steely blue eyes met her gaze directly, and his voice communicated no warmth. "I'm Nik." She glanced at me sharply.

"Nik."

"Ah, you've heard about me. All good things, of course."

"Of course." I felt the pressure on my hand tighten, and I squeezed hers quickly in return.

"Come, sit. It's late. Or early, depending on how you want to think of it. I've made coffee."

Things were uncomfortable, at best. We sat at the kitchen table. Nik's coffee was strong, like he'd always made it, and I saw Lexi grimace as she swallowed. She cleared her throat. "So, how do you and Eric know each other?" she asked.

"I noticed that the young man was in need of gainful employment. I decided I'd offer him some work."

"That was generous of you." Lexi looked at me.

"Yes. I'm the true definition of a philanthropist," he said dryly.

"It was a pretty sweet deal," Eric added, taking a swig of his drink. "Takes me off the street, lets me live here, and then pays me to find this guy." He gestured with his free hand at me. "Easiest money I ever made."

"How did you find me?"

"Easy. Nik said you like looking for money in condos way up in the air. I started reading a bunch of newspapers online from all over the place for stories about strings of high-rise robberies. I kept looking until I found the right city. And then I just watched the skies in the pricey neighborhoods. Eventually, there you were. I followed you."

"Pretty good."

"I taught him to outsmart even you, my boy." Nik smiled thinly across the table at me. "It's too bad you were so easily found."

"Not really," Eric interjected quickly. "If I hadn't found him, he probably woulda bled out."

Lexi blanched slightly, and I tried to steer the topic to lighter things. "So, how'd you find this place?"

"Bank was auctioning it off. The family all died in a tragic accident. Carbon monoxide, I think they said." So much for lighter conversation. Carbon monoxide. Right.

"So you own it?"

"I do. Free and clear. This and a dozen other properties. Bet you never thought you'd see the day when I owned my own land."

"Can't say I did."

"It's a lovely home," Lexi said.

"Home indeed." We fell, then, into an uncomfortable silence.

He drained his cup and stood abruptly. "Time to talk, Joshua. You and I."

I took Lexi's hand. "I'm not leaving her alone here," I said. I'd come to a decision at the table. "She already knows about me, obviously. Anything you plan to say can be said in front of her."

Nik tilted his head thoughtfully. "As you wish then." I was certain he saw her as a threat; he must feel that way about Eric too and, if that were true, Eric was no safer here than Lexi. I knew exactly how Nik felt about liabilities. As we settled down in the living room – Lexi and I on the couch, Nik standing awkwardly across the room against the wall – I could hear the clink of dishes as Eric began cleaning up.

Nik cleared his throat. He looked almost vulnerable, standing there, trying to figure out how to begin. I'd never seen the man look so unsure of himself. "I didn't want to leave anything unsaid."

"Is this where you tell me you've always loved me like a son?"

"No. This is where I tell you who you really are." Lexi inhaled sharply beside me, and it took me a moment to realize I was holding my breath too. He waited for us to exhale, and then he continued. "I knew your mother and father – your real ones. You might as well know – I was in love with your mother, and I was there the day you were taken." The room was so still that we could have been in a painting. A thousand questions rushed to mind, but I couldn't seem to give voice to any of them. "We used to live with others of our kind – in parts of Siberia, up in the mountain caves. Ours is one tribe of many. Your mother and I –" He hesitated and then seemed to decide something. "There's a much easier way to do this." He crossed the room, stopping directly in front of me.

"Do what?"

"Make you understand where you came from."

He placed his hand on my cheek. "What…" I started, but I felt the question die in my throat as a rush of memories flooded my senses. The sharp scent of trees, the cool winter air, the drifting snow – and her. I could see her in my mind as clearly as I saw Nik standing before me. She grinned, her dark familiar eyes gleaming at me in the twilight and her wings extending from the back of her white fur tunic.

Except she wasn't really looking at me, I realized. These were

Nik's memories. She was looking at him. Together, they were flying downwards towards a low, white clearing, far below the snow-capped mountaintops. Nik was flying.

"What's happening?" Lexi's voice was panicked.

I couldn't look away from Nik's face, but she was waiting for some kind of answer. I groped for words to explain what was happening. "I'm pretty sure I can see Nik's memories."

"How?" she asked.

"Pay attention," Nik whispered to me, ignoring Lexi. In his thoughts, he and my mother landed amid trees. She was holding a small bundle securely against her body with one hand and, with her other, she touched his. I could feel, through the emotion in his thoughts, how much he loved her. There was an air of excitement about them, too: a thrill and a newness. She looked down, her smile faltering, and I realized then that the bundle in her arms was a small baby, with eyes like hers, like mine.

"Is that me?" I asked, interrupting his vision.

He nodded. "We'd meet like this, every few days, while she was out gathering snow for water. She'd bring you, and we'd leave you in a small outcropping of rocks among the cave while we – enjoyed – each other's company. Your father didn't know."

In the memory, she placed me down on the snowy ground. My wings were fanned out around me. She took Nik's hand again, and they flew off a ways, leaving me lying there alone.

"We should never have been flying below the tree line. But the knowledge came too late." I heard my mother's scream ring out – a loud, broken sound. She grasped at the ground, frantically, clinging to the empty blanket. Nik was looking around quickly, scanning the woods and the trees. The retreating figures of two people with backpacks, a high-powered flashlight to guide their way, were just visible in the distance. Nik flew after them, leaving my mother behind him in a heap on the snow. He closed in on the couple and, with a sudden surge of speed, pushed the man to the ground. I could see, through his eyes, the fight. In the periphery, I saw a woman clutching the baby close, tears streaming down her face. She looked familiar. I knew that face. I knew that woman. Nik's attention, though, was on the man. They were fighting; Nik was powerful and angry, but the man was more sure on his feet. The ground was home to the man and foreign to Nik. Gear was everywhere, and Nik's hand was around the man's throat. I could hear the woman screaming in the background. "Let him go! Stop! Please!" They were words spoken in English. So familiar. Then I heard a loud crack, and Nik's vision went black.

"I tried so hard to get you back. But I failed. They were climbers; adventurers on some kind of pointless exposition. And we left you right in their path. They took you, Joshua. Stole you. By the time I came to, they were long gone through the woods, daylight was coming, and your mother was destroyed."

"Joshua?" Lexi's voice broke through again. "What's going on?" I blinked quickly and moved my head back, away from Nik's touch.

"I'm sorry, Lexi," I said, feeling like I couldn't even quite catch my breath, feeling ashamed for shutting Lexi out completely. "I just – Nik was *showing* me my mother. My real one."

"Showing you?" Her eyes were wide as she studied my face. "How?"

I looked at Nik and repeated the question. "How?"

"We –and others like us – have abilities that they – " he steadied a pointed gaze at Lexi, "don't."

"Like?" I asked.

"Like flight, as you know, and the ability to see without light. Like our preference and tolerance for cold extremes. We need less sleep; we heal faster." He looked back at me and shrugged. "These things you know, of course. But we can also share memories, images, and emotions with others like ourselves, at will. Our energies connect through skin contact."

Lexi's brow furrowed, and she opened her mouth to ask another question, but then closed it again. "Nik used to be like me." I told her. Her gaze shifted to my wings and then back to my face. "What are we?" I asked the question for her.

"Human, or so I've been told. Whether it's adaptation or mutation, we don't really know. We just know that they," he gestured to Lexi again, "don't like it. So we stay hidden."

"What happened after they took me?"

"The climbers lost one of their backpacks in the scuffle. It contained the woman's passport. We couldn't read it, of course. Despite what Americans think, English is not a universally known language. But there was a clear picture of her, and I knew it was only a matter of time until I figured out what the markings on the paper meant. When we met with the council, they made the unanimous decision that going after you was not an option. The likelihood of finding you was so slight, and the risk of exposure of our kind too great. Instead, the action we took was to move deeper into the mountains, find new, more remote caves, hope they couldn't trace your existence back to us. So we moved. Your mother was never the same after you disappeared."

"And my father?"

"He could barely bring himself to speak to her at first. But your siblings needed him – and her." Brothers. Sisters. Family. "So I offered to go after you, to find you. She knew I could never bring you back, since it was forbidden even to look for you. But the idea that I would find you, protect you, look after you, teach you to exist among the strangers was what she needed to be able to continue living. And I think it also helped her to have me leave. So I had my wings removed." In a fluid motion, he turned and pulled up his shirt, revealing the white, jagged scars along his emaciated back. Removed. The thought had never even occurred to me, so natural a part of me were they. To suddenly be unable to fly must have been unbearable. How had he adjusted to sudden life on the ground?

"You did that for me?"

He shook his head. "For your mother. And it took a very long time for me to fulfill my promise to her. After I had made my way through Russia, I didn't even know where else to begin. I had nothing but that passport. So I systematically traced every rumor, every snatch of hearsay, every single local legend or hint of a sighting. I lived in the shadows and moved at night. I learned more languages in a year than most people do in a lifetime. Eventually, I found myself in the middle of nowhere, USA. Eleven years after I had started looking, there you were. The explorer and his wife had smuggled you out of Russia, brought you home, and kept you, like some kind of pet."

"Child," I said softly.

"Prisoner! Don't fool yourself with sentimentality. You were forbidden to use your wings. Did you know you had never flown until you met me? They'd made you forget who you were and hide what you are. I gave my wings to find you; they'd taught you to pretend you didn't even have yours!"

I was remembering, now, the woman without wings who brought me up as her own; I saw her smiling brown eyes with laugh lines around the edges – my mother. I touched his arm, almost automatically. I could hear her voice in my head and, as I listened, I knew he could hear it too. *In the great green room, there was a telephone* – Good Night Moon. She'd read it every night to me, before bed. It was the strangest feeling – listening to the hate in Nik's voice, feeling it vibrate through him, while, at the same time, knowing he could feel with me the warmth of my blue comforter wrapped around my body and hear with me the soothing tenor of my mother's voice. *Good night, Joshua. I love you.*

Nik shook me off violently. "Don't you understand? I couldn't let them get away with it." I reached out to touch him again, to show him how soft her touch was when she dried my tears after a nightmare, when she brushed my hair from my face. He had to understand. His thoughts overpowered mine, and I saw them, mixed with my own sudden memories. Flames, now. Thick smoke. Nik's eyes, filled with blind fury. My father's strong arms, carrying me through the building, shielding me with his body from the falling debris. And then, my mother's frantic hands, pulling me from his grasp, lifting me through the side window and, as my feet touched the gravel driveway outside, pushing me, her urgent voice instructing me to run, run. Don't stop; don't look back. Run. I heard the screams behind me as I ran until my legs ached, my lungs burned, and my body finally collapsed in the snow. I remembered lying there, under the stars, my hands clasped tightly over my ears, trying to shut out the sound of terror that I'd left behind me. My world finally faded. When I awoke, Nik was there, standing over me. I didn't recognize him at all, and my life before that point was suddenly shrouded from my mind. I'd believed every lie he'd told me since then.

Sick, I swallowed my horror. I'd run away and left them to die. And then, what was worse, I allowed the murderer to teach me, to raise me, to take their place.

"You killed my family." I spoke without emotion, not asking a question, just stating a fact.

"Not your family. Not your *real* family. And *they* were the ones who killed *you*. Took you, made you hide, made you forget, made you afraid of your own abilities." He touched my shoulder again, the heat repulsive this time. "They didn't deserve to live."

I was on my feet then, my hands around his throat, pinning him against the wall. He didn't even attempt to resist, his hollow eyes looking unflinchingly into mine as my grasp tightened.

13

"Joshua!" Her voice penetrated my rage, and I could feel her hands pulling weakly at my arms. "Joshua, let go. Please. You're killing him!" There was fear in her voice, panic. "You're not like him. You're not." I watched the color draining from his face as he continued to look levelly at me, his memories becoming foggy, unclear. His eyes were beginning to roll. I released my grip, pulling my hands away abruptly. She was wrong, of course. I was exactly like him.

His face was composed as he calmly stood and caught his breath. As sick and as frail as he was, he was still stronger than I. He had never been weak. After he regained his composure, he simply straightened his shirt and asked, "Are you done?"

I wanted to stalk out, to leave, to take Lexi back home to where she was safe and surrounded by her own family, to just continue my meaningless existence. But he'd changed everything now. No matter how I felt about him and what he'd done and what he'd made me, the fact was, there were others out there like me. Family. Answers.

"So how do I get back?" I finally asked. "Is it possible?"

"Not with her." He gestured dismissively to Lexi.

"No." As hurtful as it would be for her to hear me say it, I was in agreement with him. How could I bring her with me? It wouldn't be safe for her. It wouldn't be right. It hadn't been right to bring her with me this far. I would never endanger her like this again.

"It's a long way, too. Especially if you intend to fly."

"I'm used to it. I've been all over."

"I am aware," Nik said. "I'm the one who taught you to keep moving." I had so many other questions.

Instead, I said, "Show me how."

He did. We sat on the couch and he reached out and took my hands. He showed me first my home: tall mountaintops and, within the deep caverns, many single, dark dwellings, their door openings covered by thick leather curtains. I saw winged inhabitants that walked within the dwellings and flew without, high in the air, among and above the mountains. Then, in my mind, he slowly and carefully showed me his memories of a map he'd created, from the edge of Siberia into the mountain territories, to where I would find the caves in which they dwelt. The map was sketched in my mind's eye and it was perfect. He went over the wordless instructions again, as Lexi watched our silent exchange quietly. Then he rose and headed out of the room. "Goodnight, Joshua," he said, without turning. "Help yourself to food for the journey. You'll need enough for ten days. Eric will show you to your room now." As he passed through the kitchen, he inclined his head towards Eric, who opened the cupboard for me and stood waiting against the counter.

They'd thought ahead. There were bottles of water, stacks of granola bars, and cans of food with pull tabs. I'd need enough to last me, but it would have to fit in my bag – and it couldn't weigh me down too much. I filled the pack carefully with as little as I could. Enough for survival, nothing more. As I zipped it up, Eric gestured. I straightened, taking Lexi's hand wordlessly and following him.

I considered leaving immediately – grabbing my still-packed bag and starting out right away. It was already dark, and I was eager to get away from this place, from Nik, and from the way I hated him. But before I'd even finished the thought, I knew, without a shadow of doubt, that, before I could set out, I would need to have Lexi safely on her way back home. Eric would need to be safe too. Whether he realized it or not, he knew enough to make himself a threat to Nik, and I was aware of how Nik dealt with threats. I would need to take both of them with me and put enough distance between them and Nik to let me believe they would be safe. I tried to keep my expression neutral as Eric led us down the short, narrow hallway.

As nice as it would have been to have forgiven Nik, nothing had changed. In fact, his confessions had only made it worse. I knew him now to be even less of a human being than I had previously thought.

He had given us a room on the main floor. Outside the open door, Eric paused. "Will you two be – sharing a room?" I wasn't planning on leaving her alone, even for a moment, never mind all night. I noted, with some satisfaction, that he looked disappointed when I nodded. When we were alone in our room, I felt Lexi shift beside me, uneasily. I followed her gaze to the double bed in the middle of the room. We'd lain in her bed together before, but it had never felt so serious.

"So, should I make up my bed on the floor?" I asked, trying to keep my tone light.

She colored slightly. "I'm sure we can share this bed without ... complicating things."

I made the first move into the room and sat on the bed. Feigning nonchalance, I pulled off my shoes. She sat beside me. "What are you going to do now?" she asked.

"Now? I guess now I'm going to try to get some sleep."

"You know that's not what I meant."

"I know. I guess I'm going to find them. You know, right, that I can't take you with me? But I can't leave you here, either."

"Why not? If you're just going to take off anyway, what difference does it make?" I knew she was trying to sound casual, but she couldn't take the bite out of her tone. "I'm sure Eric will give me a ride back." She emphasized his name, trying to strike at me with it.

"He could. But I'm not sure how much I trust him, either. And besides, everything I know about Nik tells me that I can't be leaving anyone here with him, considering how much you two know." I felt her shudder beside me.

"You really think he's capable of that?"

"I know he is. You do too."

She nodded, touching my arm. "I'm sorry about your parents."

"Thanks."

"You really don't need to do this alone." There was no sense in me arguing with her. She was wrong, of course. I didn't even know where I was going, exactly. And when I got there, I didn't know what would happen. She had the whole world at her fingertips. How could I ever let her give any of it up for something as uncertain as this? I didn't tell her how much I wanted her to come with me, though, how much it killed me to turn her down. I imagined what it would feel like to have her in my arms as I flew towards this new life, to feel her body beside me each time I lay down to rest. It wouldn't make it any easier for her to know how much I actually cared about her. It wouldn't help her to know that, for the briefest moment, when I realized Nik had had his wings removed, I'd almost envied him. "Do you believe him? About everything?"

I nodded slowly. "I remember now. Not the stuff from before, not my life with my real family. But growing up. My mom and dad. The place we lived. I remember everything. And I remember the night Nik attacked us. The night he took everything from me." I looked towards the door, thinking again about Nik. "We'll get somewhere safe before I go."

She gestured now to her small bag, crammed full with her clothes and accessories. "I'm going to get changed." She let the statement hang in the air. I was tempted to make myself comfortable. I suspected she wouldn't object.

Instead, I nodded quickly. "I'll wait outside the room." I left and closed the door behind me, leaning against the cool wall in the hallway. Nik was up. I could see him in the leather recliner in the living room. His head was turned and he was staring blankly out the window. As if he sensed my eyes on him, he shifted his gaze to mine.

"So you two aren't together?"

"I don't know. Maybe. But not like you mean."

"She's not bad looking, I'll give you that. But where you're from, there are beauties I can't even describe to you, both in your village and the neighboring ones. You'll be glad you returned unattached." I rebelled inwardly at his words, but they held appeal for me at the same time. I'd never thought of the possibility of meeting a woman who was like me, who wouldn't see me as strange or exotic or exciting, except for the fact that I'd lived far away for so long. A woman of my own *kind.* Still, I couldn't shake the feeling that I was losing something far more valuable in Lexi. Even when I'd lied to her about the wings, I'd never lied to her about who I was. And she didn't love me because of the wings, nor in spite of them. She just loved me.

I was pretty sure that I would always hate Nik but, as I stood there, looking at the dying man sitting alone in the darkened living room, I didn't. "Thanks for the truth," I told him, meaning it.

I heard Lexi call my name. Nik inclined his head. "Good night, Joshua."

"Goodnight." I returned to the room. Lexi was waiting. She

was sitting on the bed, pretending to read, with her legs under the thick comforter. She was dressed in the pale blue nightshirt I'd seen her in a number of times before. I had never noticed how extraordinarily fine she looked wearing it, how the neckline flowed along her collar bone, how the thin fabric hugged the curves of her slender shoulders, how the blue hue made her skin look even more creamy white than it already did. It was difficult for me to tear my gaze away, but she seemed to be making such a valiant effort to look relaxed that I felt I should follow suit. "If you don't mind, I'll slide in beside you, although I'm not sure I'll sleep." Her head shot up, eyes wide, cheeks pink with the unintended implication. "I mean – because it's night. I don't usually sleep at night," I rushed to explain. "And we won't be staying the whole night. "

"Oh. Sure." She looked embarrassed.

Since I wasn't planning to sleep, undressing was unnecessary. Saying goodbye would be difficult enough as it was. If I let myself feel any more than I already did, it just might be impossible. Fully clothed, I slid into the bed beside her. She put her book away and we turned, lying on our sides simultaneously, to face one another. She rested her cold feet on mine. I knew she could hardly make out my face in the dark of the room, but she smiled at me. "I can't believe this will be our last night together."

"I know."

"Will you miss me?"

"Yes." I didn't know if it would be enough for her. She reached out her hand in the darkness and rested her palm on my face. It was.

"You're a good man, Joshua. No matter what you've done or how you feel about yourself," she said, tracing my mouth with her thumb. "I've been lucky to know you."

"You know I'm the lucky one," I said.

"You too." She moved closer and pressed her lips gently against mine. A torrent of emotions ran through me at the touch of her mouth. Gratefulness. Loss. But most of all, consuming need. I deepened the kiss and wrapped my arms around her body, pulling her tight against me. She was so warm. I was losing control; I felt it slipping away, even as I realized we had to stop. I turned my face, pulling back breathlessly and moving my lips away from hers. This wasn't fair to her, and the loss would be unbearable to me if I let it go any further.

Wordlessly, she turned onto her back and, after I rolled onto my stomach, she moved to lie again against my body, our arm and leg touching.

We lay like that, my wings fanned out over our bodies, heads turned towards one another, until her eyelids grew heavy and she had to fight to keep her eyes open. "I like being here with you Joshua. It feels safe."

"It is safe." It was my promise to her. She didn't miss it.

"I know." She reached up now, carefully running her fingertips along the body of my wings. "They're really beautiful. I can't believe I ever thought they weren't part of you."

"Sometimes, I wish they weren't, although I can't imagine having them removed like Nik did."

"I think it would be sad," she said. "No wonder he was so angry."

"It was his choice to get them removed."

"I know. But it must have hurt him every time you flew and he couldn't. I see how you are when we're up there. It's where you're most at home."

"It *is* where I'm most at home," I said, "there, and right here, with you."

"Me too. You'll always have a home with me." She ran her hand along the wings to my shoulder and down my arm. Her hand moved to rest on mine, and we lay like that until her eyes drifted close and her breathing became deep and rhythmic. Eventually, I got up, careful not to move the bed too much and waken her. I quietly packed up. We'd be gone before Nik awoke in the morning.

It didn't take long for me to ready our things. Sitting on the edge of the bed, I marvelled how one person could come to mean so much to me.

At four o'clock, it was time to go. I ran my hand gently along her arm. Her eyelids fluttered open, and she blinked at me and offered a slow smile. "Time to go already?"

"Yep."

She blinked again and sat up. "It's still dark. Are we all packed?"

"Mm-hmm."

"Are we bringing Eric?"

"We are. Just be ready, okay?" I padded quickly down the hall until I stood outside Eric's room. The door was open, and he lay sprawled across his bed, snoring. Waking him was a gamble. If he were loyal to Nik, he'd wake him and leaving would be messy. I risked it anyway. "Eric." Louder. "Eric."

His eyes opened to slits. "Who's there?"

"Who do you think?"

He sighed. "What's going on?"

"I thought I'd let you know Lexi and I are leaving now."

"That's it? Have a safe trip." He lay back down, heavily.

I hesitated. "Do you know anything about the man you've been working for?"

"Enough."

"Come with us. Nik doesn't like the idea of anybody getting in his way and, if he thinks you know too much, you probably don't want to be around when he doesn't need you anymore."

He was quiet, considering. "You make a good argument," he said.

"Have you unpacked already?"

"Nope. To be honest, I wasn't planning on sticking around."

The floor creaked behind me. Just Lexi. "So, are we going then?" she asked.

"Sure." Eric flung off the covers, pulled a shirt over his head, and slid on his jeans. "He's given me the cash he promised. Let's go." We left quietly, making our way down the hall and out of the front door. I noticed Eric left it ajar slightly, so the click wouldn't wake Nik.

14

We drove straight down the highway, away from the gravel road and the house and the threat of Nik. As the sky began to lighten, Eric glanced at me for the first time in the rear view mirror. "So where, exactly, are we headed?" he asked.

I'd been giving it a lot of thought. The easiest way to keep Lexi safe was to send her back home, alone. Disconnect her entirely from Eric and myself. She would be far more difficult to find on her own. "The nearest bus station," I replied.

Eric laughed, his voice loud in the cramped car. "Bus station? I really didn't figure you for a public transportation kind of guy."

"For Lexi."

"I have nowhere in particular I need to go. I could drive her. You don't trust me to get her home?"

Not by a long shot. "It's safer for both of you. It will be harder for him to track you if you're not together."

"How could that old man find us, anyway?"

"He found me, didn't he?"

"Yeah, thanks to me."

"There's always someone willing to do another person's dirty work."

"Fair enough," he said. "So we just split up and wait for him to find us?"

"We split up so he doesn't find us." I put my hand on Lexi's shoulder. "Nik doesn't know anything about Lexi – where she's from, where she lives. How much have you told him, Eric?"

"Nothing – he didn't even ask where I found you. He just wanted to know that I was bringing you back."

"And does he know where you're from?"

"I'm not really from anywhere anymore. He found me begging for change and offered to change my life. It will be easy for me to disappear."

"Nik will know that, too. Make sure, Eric, you don't go back to where he found you."

Eric was the type of guy I would have recruited as one of my contacts as well. He had nothing going for him, except us now. And even that was temporary.

"You don't have any family?" Lexi asked.

"Of course I have family. I just haven't spoken to any of them for years."

"Why not?"

"I ran away when I was thirteen. Stupid, really. I thought I would join a band, make it big in Las Vegas. It didn't happen, of course. My friends disappeared. And going back home would be humiliating. So, here I am."

"Could you go back now?"

"I don't know. Maybe. What would I say? After the things I've done?"

"Would that matter to them?"

He shrugged. "I don't know." I felt his struggle. What do you say to a family who may not even want you back?

"I know, if I lost someone I loved, I would watch for them every single day until they came home." Lexi's voice was quiet.

"I knew it would crush my mom when I took off. I didn't care.

Figured she'd just get over it. Maybe she has already."

"Bet she hasn't," Lexi said. "I'd go back, if I were you."

"It's what you are doing," I reminded her gently.

"I know." We followed Lexi's GPS into the next city and then to the first bus depot. Lexi disappeared into the big gray building to buy a ticket home.

"And you're taking off too?" Eric asked, mostly just to fill the silence.

"Yeah. Once Lexi's gone, I'll wait in your car until night falls, if you don't mind."

Lexi swung open the door and sat back down, bus ticket in hand. She craned around in her seat to look at me. "You're really going to do this on your own?"

"I need to," I said.

"I'd go with you, you know. In a heartbeat."

"I know."

Eric cleared his throat uncomfortably. "This is getting a little awkward. I'm gonna go get something to eat, okay?" When neither of us responded, he sighed and left the car, closing the door gently behind him.

"I'm in love with you, you know," she said. "I really am."

"I know."

"I've never felt anything like this, for anyone. And now I don't think I could love anyone else." I didn't respond, and I wasn't sure if she wanted me to. Instead, I just looked at her, this amazing girl with the fiery red hair and dark purple contacts. I noticed her roots were starting to grow in. Strawberry blonde.

"You'll be fine," I said. I didn't offer any sentiments of my own. She had known how this was going to end.

"Joshua?" she said, after a moment.

"Yeah?"

"What if it doesn't work out?"

I didn't ask her what she meant. There were dozens of ways

I could fail. I might not be able to find them. They might have moved. They might not welcome me back.

"Then I'll move on, I guess. Figure out what to do next when I get there."

"I'll be watching for you, you know."

"You shouldn't."

"I know. But I will. All this stuff – my life, my home, my friends – none of it really matters. I would give it up for you in a second."

"I would never ask you to do that."

"You wouldn't need to ask. I'm just telling you that I would. You'll always have a home with me, if you want it."

"Okay." What else could I say? The interior light clicked on as Eric swung open the door and hopped in, a tray of drinks and a bag of food in his arms.

"You guys done?" he asked, rhetorically. "Good. I'm hungry and tired of feeling uncomfortable. Food." He placed the drink tray on the center console and tossed a turkey sandwich at me. As I unwrapped the plastic, he handed one to Lexi and opened his own. As we ate, he grabbed two napkins and wrote something down on each of them. He handed one to me and one to Lexi. "It's my parents' number," he said. "In case things don't work out there and you wanna look me up. I'd give you my cell number, but I ditched the phone back there with Nik. Just in case."

We settled in to wait, and too soon, it was time for her to go. Without a word, she got out of the car, walked around to the trunk, and pulled out her bag. Eric motioned to help, but she waved him off. Then, to my surprise, she came around to my door, pulled it open, and crawled in tight beside me. Eric looked pointedly out his window. "If you change your mind, you know where to find me." She pressed her lips against mine. And then she was gone, through the glass doors leading to the bus terminal.

We waited until the bus pulled away, and I saw her at the window, palm flat against the glass, looking unwaveringly at our car until I could no longer make her out. We watched until the bus disappeared around the corner, and then we continued sitting, staring at the empty street. Finally, Eric settled back into his seat. "Are you good to go? Or did you want to wait for nightfall here?"

"No, let's drive. The more distance between one another, the better." As we set out, I stared at the passing city, then at the fields. I could still taste her lips on mine. Eric wasn't in a talkative mood, and I was grateful for the fact. I knew I'd have a lot of time for solitary thought in the future, and maybe I should have wanted to use this fleeting time for conversation or companionship, but I didn't have anything more I wanted to say.

As the sun disappeared over the horizon, I knew it was time to set out on my own. I tapped Eric's shoulder. He glanced briefly at me in the mirror and then pulled onto the shoulder of the highway. I waited until a convoy of trucks had passed us and the night was quiet and still. My bag was already at my feet, and I picked it up. I got out of the car. My wings were ready – I could feel their energy as I thought about being in the sky again. I leaned in once more. "Thanks for the ride."

"No problem, Man. It's been interesting. Good luck with – whatever."

"Thanks. And don't look back, okay?"

"Don't plan to."

I slammed the door and walked out into the field. I watched his car peel away and the taillights disappear down the long, flat stretch of highway. Then I was up, in the air, above the beautiful mess of the world.

Nik's instructions had been clear. From just outside of Colorado to the mountains in Siberia, Russia, it would be close to 4800 miles. I couldn't cross directly over the ocean – it would be too long a flight without a place to land. I'd have to go up through Wyoming and Idaho, cross into Canada, and then fly through to

Alaska. Then there would be a short stint over the ocean before hitting Russia. If I managed to fly ten hours a day – and I was pretty sure I could do it, as long as I found places to crash during the daylight hours when I was passing cities – it would take me ten days, flying at a quick pace.

I watched the landscape fade beneath me. I knew much of the way by heart. There were very few places in the world my wings hadn't taken me, and navigating the skies was instinctive; it always had been. I used to be surprised at how easily I recognized landmarks and specific areas.

Getting there went fairly smoothly. It rained the first day of my journey. By the seventh day, it was snowing. Shaving was impossible and, by the time I crossed the ocean, I'd actually managed to grow a beard. It was a new feeling for me, like I'd aged years, rather than just over a week. I hadn't ever tried to let it grow before.

When I finally arrived in Russia, I'd finished the little food I'd packed. The air, up in the Siberian mountains, was cooler than I was used to, but I wasn't cold. Nik had been right; this was home. As I reached the untouched wilderness and let my wings carry me higher into the mountains, it was as if my body knew the way. I could *feel* myself getting closer, like home was calling to me.

Finally, on the edges of the horizon, I could make out a small outcropping of caves like Nik had described. Nearing them, I scanned the sky for motion, and then turned to focus on the ground below. No signs of any life.

I landed at the entrance of the one nearest me. Still, silent. "Hello?" I called out into the cavern. "Is anyone here?" I stepped inside, out from the light of the early evening and into the black of the cave. My eyes took a moment to adjust. As the contours of the walls and ground slowly took shape, I couldn't see any evidence of life outside of a few small creatures peering out at me from the shadows. "Hello?" I called once more and stopped to listen. Nothing.

I walked back out into the snow outside, my legs feeling heavy. I was more exhausted than I'd realized and it was so peaceful outside. I sat, leaning against the cool of the rock, and looked out into the orange sky. I'd come so close. The snow started to fall, and I closed my eyes. When I opened them again, it was dark, and I was surrounded.

15

I blinked again and five young faces came sharply into focus. A boy, with two girls on either side of him, leaned in close to me, speaking loudly in a language I didn't recognize, one I'd never heard spoken before. The cadence and rhythm was unfamiliar, the word breaks unrecognizable in a flow of syllables and sounds from deep in the throat.

I struggled to my feet, my legs still stiff with sleep, and the children stepped back abruptly. Their fur tunics, leather boots, and long translucent wings affirmed what my instincts had been telling me since I'd neared this place – I'd found my way home.

The children fell silent as the boy extended his right hand, using the other to brush a brown strand of hair from his eyes. He hesitated, his hand hovering just beside my cheek. I nodded, once, and he pressed his palm to my face.

Nothing happened. I'd been expecting to be flooded with memories like I had been with Nik. Instead, the boy just looked at me, waiting.

"You want my memories?" I asked. I had no idea how to show him anything. I'd been able to show Nik a memory, but it had been an accident. I had no idea how to control it. I'd been away from them my whole life.

The boy replied, his words little more than an assortment of sounds to me. The rest were quiet, their gazes unwavering. Still waiting.

I closed my eyes, picturing the Manhattan Skyline, the light from the towers and citadels illuminating the night. In my memory, I navigated the sky just above and then, on impulse, swooped down to pass close beside the spire of the One World Tower. The air was cool and, although I'd seen it dozens of times, the vibrant tapestry still took my breath away.

The boy dropped his hand and when I opened my eyes he'd already grasped the hands of the girls on either side of him, who linked their hands with the two girls beside them. A murmur of sound passed between them. He was undoubtedly sharing my memory with them. When he returned his hand to my face, he was still linked with the children on his left, and the girl on his right moved forward to touch his arm. A sense of wonder, so strong it was almost palpable, radiated from them. They'd never seen a cityscape before.

"You like that?" I asked. "You'll love this." I envisioned San Francisco now, remembering the last time I navigated that sky, weaving slowly through the maze of skyscrapers. I'd been on my way back to my apartment but, as I neared the Golden Gate Bridge, I gave into a rare impulse and wound my way down to the top of the red tower. I landed on the edge of the platform. Although the lanes below were alive with the sound of late night traffic, the moment was one of peace, with the wind teasing the tips of my wings and the lights from the bridge cables refracting off the still water below.

Without meaning to, I thought of Lexi. She would have loved to see San Francisco from the sky. Her face appeared in my mind, and I could feel their emotions spike in response to mine. Reining in my thoughts, I pictured the places I'd seen with her during our last days together instead; the wide expanse of fields, the long, wild grass, the empty starlit sky.

One of the girls spoke to me, and, although I couldn't understand the words, I felt the sentiment behind them. Wonder. She said something to the boy and he nodded. A different image appeared in my mind, one I hadn't created. It was a snow-covered world, very much like the one Nik had shown me, but with a slightly different arrangement of mountains. If this were my tribe, they must have moved farther north. On the surface of the mountains were great caverns and, between their peaks, flew others like them. Like me.

I brought the face of my first mother to mind. If they were from my tribe, maybe they'd recognize her. The same image echoed back to me, only this woman was older, with graying hair and lines around her eyes. The smile was the same.

The girl who had spoken to me said something to the girl beside her. Their wings came to life, and the two rose into the air. I watched them vanish into the distance and then looked back at the boy. He nodded and showed me three men in brown tunics. On their backs, slung between each of their four, almost translucent wings, were long bows, and quivers of arrows hung at their hips. Then, he looked up and pointed. I followed his gaze. The three men he'd shown me were approaching through the darkened sky. One of them called out, a loud, wordless shout. I raised my hand in greeting.

The three landed on the snow in front of me, more gracefully than their muscled frames would have suggested possible. They spoke to the children first; after a short exchange, the children released their hands and left, rising quickly into the sky and disappearing beside the mountainside. The men turned their gazes to me again and, for the first time, I felt a flash of fear. The blond one closest me grasped my wrist, his fingers digging into my skin, and twisted me around sharply, so I found myself with my arm held tight behind me, his knees on my back, and my cheek against the snow. He barked something at me. When I didn't reply, he said it louder.

"I don't know what you're saying," I said, fighting the rising panic. "I don't speak your language."

The man shouted at me again, the pressure increasing. I couldn't inhale. The edges of my vision darkened. If I didn't do something soon, I was going to pass out. How was I supposed to explain what I was doing here when he couldn't understand me? I pictured Nik's face, when he was healthy. The pressure lessened, so I focused on the memory of Nik helping me up after the fire, when he found me in the snowy field. The man spoke again, his voice quieter but still sharp.

I showed him the Nik I knew now, the sunken cheeks and ashen complexion and frail body. I thought through the details of the visions he'd last given me; the day I was taken, the fire, and the specific way back home. I felt a wave of fear from the man who held me. I tried to project my emotions to him, the ones beyond my own distress. No harm. No danger.

The man rose, releasing me. I struggled to my feet and turned to face him. He extended his hand, and I reached out my own to grasp it. I was watching my mother and the younger Nik land flying towards the caves, carrying the empty blankets. I met his eye and nodded, laying my other hand on my chest.

He turned away abruptly, speaking rapidly to the other men. They laid their hands on his arms, and I knew he was showing them my memories. He looked again at me and pointed up to the way in which they had come. "Am I coming with you?" I asked. His wings carried him up off the ground. I followed, flanked by the others. The children hadn't returned home after all; I noticed them appear from within a nook and follow us, holding hands. We flew deeper into the mountains, around several curves and into a larger section of caves and hills. As we dipped down into a slightly lower area, I caught my breath; the sky was filled with people like me. It was exactly like I'd seen in Nik's memories, only more real and more beautiful. The place was alive at night. It was no wonder that I'd always loved the dark. There were animal pens, too, especially within the dips; sheep, pigs, chickens, cows. The men saw me looking and one of them touched my arm. I could see their uses immediately; meat and milk, just like in most places.

Finally, we landed in one of the large cave openings. They gestured for me to follow. I didn't hesitate.

The inside of the cave was ornate. There was no light. None was needed, of course, but it seemed strange to me in comparison with my former world. Beautiful paintings adorned the cave walls. The man stopped outside an opening. There were no doors, but the entrances were covered by heavy, leather drapery. The children lingered back.

I caught my breath. The drapery was moved aside and, there before us, looking slightly concerned with the presence of the watchmen at her door, stood my mother, with graying hair like the children had shown me, a slight build, fine features, and eyes the precise color of mine. After a moment, she gasped in recognition. Her eyes moistened and she blinked rapidly. I was her son; she was my mother.

It was surreal. We had no words to share, and so we stood mutely for a moment. Then she reached out her hands to me and I took them. Our skin warmed at the touch, and I saw again the empty blanket, this time from her eyes. I felt her grief as if it were my own. The image faded, and it was replaced by her memory of holding me when I was newly born, touching my soft, feathery hair, counting my toes, marveling as my hands grasped her fingers. I felt the love she'd had for me, the joy I'd given her with my birth.

In return, I showed her the happiest moments of my childhood, those that I had newly remembered: running along the farmyard, riding our horse, sitting in the grass and watching the sky. And I showed her Nik carrying me through the snow, bringing me to his home, feeding me hot soup as I struggled to remember why I wasn't with my family any more. I didn't show her that it was he who destroyed them, only that he rescued me. I showed her, at last, his illness, and I felt a wave of grief. I wanted her to know that he'd kept his promise. That he'd never stopped loving her. So I showed her how he'd given me the way home.

And then she was embracing me, my mother, my real, own mother. As I returned the hug, my fingers found the body of her wings. Like me. She was like me. She wanted me and loved me. Why then, even in the joy of the moment, did I feel incomplete?

She leaned away now, placing her hands on either side of my cheeks, looking into my face. She tapped my nose and then hers. We were so alike. She gestured to my eyes and then pointed to hers. Yes, I nodded. The same. I touched her shoulder. "Mother," I said. She tilted her head thoughtfully. "Mother," I said again. She was looking at my lips, and, after hearing the word again, she tried valiantly to echo the sound. And then she laughed, pulling me again into her arms. Laughter was universal.

She touched the shoulder of one of the watchman, and he nodded and exited the room. They weren't pleased to see me. The other two followed. I thought of ways to ask where they'd gone, but before I could formulate a thought, she took my hand. The face of a grinning adolescent boy appeared, his deep brown eyes sparkling at some joke. He looked like my mother. Like me, too, except for the nose. "Teket," she said. It was the first clear word I'd heard, and the first time I'd understood. My brother's name.

"Teket," I echoed, and she smiled, squeezing my hand gently. She showed me the next image; a woman, older than I, a younger and fairer version of my mother.

"Sakari," she said. My sister. She touched her own chest with her free hand. "Aanaq. Mo-ther." She placed her hand on my chest.

"Joshua," I said, trying to speak as clearly and slowly as possible. She didn't respond so I tried more slowly. "Joshua."

"Iuik." She said. She tapped her hand on my chest again. "Iuik." My name. Of course. The ones who took me from her called me Joshua. To her, I was Iuik.

I laid my hand over hers, meeting her eyes. "Iuik," I repeated.

The covering for the cave was pushed aside and a boy appeared, the one with my eyes and my unmistakable features. "Teket," I said, trying the name. He tentatively took my hand. A swell of emotions from him; excitement, fear, uncertainty. I released his hand and pulled him into a tight hug. *My brother.*

I heard the thick curtains move again, and I looked up to see the watchmen enter, this time followed by a slight woman with a fine nose and lips and eyes just like ours. My hand was finding hers without even thinking about it. *Sister. My sister.* "Sakari," I said. It sounded familiar and strange at the same time.

"Iuik." Her eyes sparkled as I broadened the hug and enfolded her in our arms. And then, we were laughing and crying. As my sister's hands touched my back, I could see her memory of me – my tiny chubby legs, the light sound of my laughter, my baby gurgles. She'd been a doting big sister; I could feel it in every thought and memory she sent to me. My disappearance, I was quickly coming to see, had been devastating to the whole family. Unlike the memories I offered to my mother, I hid the memories of my childhood from my brother and sister. I didn't think, as I stood encircled by the arms of my family, that my adoptive parents had had any idea what they were doing when they took me away from all this. They had found a lost child and rescued him. I had to believe that about them. But, in truth, they hadn't rescued me at all. No wonder Nik had been so angry.

"My father?" I asked. When nobody responded, I showed them the image of him that Nik had given me.

My mother touched my face. I saw him, older now, laying on

a low bed. He was surrounded by his family and the look on his face was one of complete peace. I was too late. I thought it even as she showed me next a plot of earth. He'd died before I'd gotten a chance to meet him. Instead of complete sorrow, though, I felt from them, unmistakably, a sense of hope. I suspected that, like so many others, they didn't see death as the final goodbye.

Eventually, we broke contact and I slowly straightened. My mother said something to me, but unlike the names, it was a long string of guttural, unfamiliar sounds.

"I'm sorry," I said, "I don't understand." Teket and Sakari gasped. My language was no pleasanter to them. My mother spoke to them and gestured for me to come farther into the dwelling. I followed her past another hanging divider and found myself in a small kitchen, with what looked like a round wooden table in the center of the room. Of course. Another universal. Food.

Lying in the soft bed, I breathed in the quiet cool of the early morning. After dinner, they'd wanted to know everything about me. I showed them some of the happier parts: the view from the city skyscrapers, the easy moments with Nik, the childhood feeling of grass between my toes. I kept the darker parts of me hidden. The thought of my family knowing who I was – someone who spent years victimizing strangers – without remorse – made me sick. I hadn't even realized before that I was ashamed.

I didn't only hold back those memories though. I didn't let them see Lexi. She was the only part of the past that made letting go painful. They didn't need to know how, even as I held my family close, I ached for her.

I closed my eyes. I could almost feel her – the warmth of her breath and the silk of her skin against mine. She would have loved this place. To see the sky filled with others like me. To meet my family. To fly over miles of white mountains.

Of course, she wouldn't fit in here anymore than I did in

the city. The constant cold, the dark, the lack of the very things she needed.

She's the past, I reminded myself. Like my other mother and father. Like my life in the city. This is what I've been looking for my entire life. Lexi has no part in it. I was lucky they'd let me back in. They hadn't had to. It was a calculated risk for the watchmen, for this community. But they risked it because I belonged.

The unsettled feeling, I believed, was just the newness of everything. I was sure that, once I'd adjusted to being here, everything would feel right. I'd forget about whatever life was like before; it would seem only a poorer version of reality.

The thick fur bedding was soft and warm. It wasn't necessary, but it was nice. As sleep claimed me, I thought I could hear Lexi whispering goodnight.

16

Evening came, and when I awoke, I could tell I'd been asleep for too long. My body was stiff from inaction, although it finally felt rested. The silence was unbroken by the sound of movement.

A thick brown tunic was lying across the foot of the bed. I shed my jeans and the layers I had slept in and pulled on the dress of my people.

As I crossed the threshold of my room and entered the kitchen, the scent of something warm filled the cave, bringing back memories of my childhood on the farm. I'd forgotten what it felt like to wake to a hot breakfast. On the low table sat a solitary clay dish, with what looked like a mixture of eggs and meat. Steam still rose from the surface. I walked through the kitchen to the outer room and moved the curtain aside slightly. My mother was just disappearing into the throngs of people moving towards the exit. I wondered for a moment if this was some sort of evacuation, but nobody seemed in a great rush to get out.

Letting the curtains fall closed, I wandered back into the kitchen and sat, feeling self-conscious. As I ate, I wondered what they did vocationally here, and how I would help. I had no real skills. I'd never learned anything useful for living as part of a real society –

nothing that would help me fit in. Would they see through me – see that I'd been nothing but a thief? I finished eating and stared down at my dish. I assumed I needed to clean this now, but I wasn't quite sure how to do even that much.

The curtain moved aside and my mother came through. She spoke to me, but stopped halfway through and put her hand on my shoulder instead. I felt a rush of joy from her, paired with an image of the empty blanket in her arms and then my appearance at her door. She never thought she would see me again. And here I was. I wished I could echo back the same emotion. I was happy to be home, but part of me was still back in America.

"Thanks for breakfast," I said, changing the topic. She didn't need the words; my recent memory of its discovery was enough. She smiled and bent down to gather the empty dish. As she moved past me, the heavy door flap was moved aside and Sakari came through, already grinning.

She said something to me and then laughed at herself. Stepping forward, she extended her hand. I took it and she pulled me up, even as she flashed me an image of myself standing at the doorway to our dwelling, watching the people rushing by.

"Where were they going?" I asked. Again, she didn't need words. She flashed an image of a long line of people, working on repairing the animal fencing. She emphasized the strength of the structure. It had to be strong enough to keep out wildlife.

The image shifted, and I saw Teket and other kids his age, gathered around an older man, who was speaking emphatically to them. Teaching them.

Another shift, and we were flying towards a large cave. Inside was breathtaking. I'd never seen anything like it. The sheer expanse of created fields was incredible. Even within caverns, life grew. It astonished me, that in such a cold climate, nature had given them a way of providing for their needs. The cave had a number of openings along the top and upper sides, allowing sunlight in. I could feel, through her, that the cave was warm inside, geothermally heated by a series of natural hot springs flowing within. Everything was primitive, yet advanced in a way I'd never imagined.

This is where they were going. To work. Sakari pulled on my hand. She wanted me to follow her. I nodded, allowing her to lead me through the darkened cave and out into the night. I almost expected to see pinpoints of light below me. Of course, there were none. Seeing the world around me, so alive in the darkness, I thought again of Nik. He'd taught me to work in the night because it was most discreet. It was the same reason they worked in the dark now. It was far less likely we'd be seen by the light of the moon and stars than by the harsh light of day. It was also, though, in our make-up. Maybe thousands of years of needing to hide had developed in us the uncanny ability to see in the dark. Maybe that explained the steadfast preference for night over day.

We spent most of the night touring the rest of the village. The cave that my family lived in wasn't the only one with homes. There were a number of others like it, home to families like ours. The layout reminded me of apartment blocks, without the locks and solid doors and security. They trusted each other here. I wondered if it was due to the community they'd built over the years or the fact that they could see one another's memories. It was obviously still possible to deceive – after all, my mother and Nik had done it for years.

People were excited to meet me. Word had spread quickly – Iuik had returned. When I showed them the world I knew – high-rises and cityscapes – I felt from them a mixture of wonder and repulsion. It could have been the crowded streets or the smell of the city air or the concrete structures shaping the skyline but, whatever it was, they didn't see the same beauty in it that I always had. They loved this cold, mountainous, secluded place. No amount of sparkling lights could dampen that.

As the sky began lightening, my sister pointed in the direction of home, and we joined the others heading back in for daylight. As we landed in the entrance, my sister tugged my hand, pulling me with her as she weaved her way through the crowded hall.

"Kaya!" she called at a retreating figure, whose straight black hair hung down to the fringe of her brown tunic. The girl turned, looking over the heads between us, and people flowed around her as she made her way back. Sakari released my hand and hurried to meet her.

"Sakari." The girl's voice was light and feminine as she took my sister's hand and said something else to her in their language. She fixed her black eyes on me as she spoke, her cheeks dimpling when she smiled. At my height, she was taller than most of the women who passed us.

Sakari answered her and, when I heard my own name, I offered a mild wave. The girl's smile widened and she reached out and laid her hand on my arm.

"Iuik," she said, meeting my eyes warmly. Her emotions were a blend of curiosity and attraction. Her cheeks colored. She'd read the same from me.

I cleared my throat. "Hi. Kaya, right?" I asked.

"Kaya," she echoed. With her free hand, she mimicked my wave. "Hi."

Sakari laughed beside me, reaching out and laying her hand on my arm. We could see ourselves from her perspective, Kaya and I standing, awkwardly frozen, in the middle of the crowded passageway. No wonder people were staring. Kaya dropped her hand, her cheeks flushing a deeper pink. Sakari spoke to her again and this time I tried to pay attention. If I were going to live here, I'd have to learn the language eventually. The sounds themselves were so unfamiliar though, and everything seemed to blend together into a single, long word.

Kaya replied and waved at me again before quickly disappearing. Sakari took my hand. She led me back to our own entrance but, as she did, she sent me images. Sakari was kneeling in the gardens of the geothermal caves. Beside her knelt a raven-haired girl in a dark brown tunic, her body curved naturally towards the ground and her hands moving the dirt aside almost tenderly. Kaya. A small smile lit her expression as she worked. They both loved it. I could see in their faces and feel it through Sakari. Kaya looked up affectionately at the person working beside her, her black eyes shimmering in the dark. I nudged Sakari and grinned when I realized Kaya was looking directly at me, and I was kneeling in the dirt beside her. I'd never worked the earth, not here or ever before. Sakari was showing me her hope for the future.

As she pushed aside the heavy curtain, Sakari's images dissipated with the welcome scent of dinner. We were home.

The next night, I didn't oversleep. I knew, without being told, that Sakari was going to take me to the cave gardens. She and Kaya worked there, and she was hoping I would too.

As we flew towards the cave after breakfast, the night sky alive with others like me, I wondered if the sight would ever feel commonplace.

We entered the cave and I was surprised to see Kaya waiting at the door for us. Sakari said something to her and then touched my arm, showing me she intended to start work without me. Kaya would show me around. I nodded to her. She shot Kaya a quick smile and left us.

"Hey Kaya," I said.

"Hey. Hi," she said, trying both greetings she'd heard from me.

"Yeah. Both are right." She wrinkled her nose at me. I got the impression she wasn't enthralled with the sound of the English language. I tried to elaborate. "Hey Kaya. Hi Kaya. Hello Kaya. Howdy Kaya. What's up, Kaya."

Laughing, she took my hand, stopping me. "Iuik," she said, her voice soft and genuine. Hearing my name from her lips was more effective than all the greetings I could think of.

Then, leading the way, she became my tour guide, going before me through rows upon rows of produce and grain. People were working: harvesting, planting, pruning, turning the soil. Pockets of workers did dayshift work, but most worked in the dark of night. She showed me, through her thoughts, how they brought earth from the valley below them. Their watchmen travelled low enough to take fresh soil in the spring, when the ground in the valley was softest.

When I saw the image of the hand tools used to till the ground and fill the holes, I showed her some of the tractors and combines I'd seen on farms, from above. She cringed at the noise from the engines and the sound of the tires over the ground. My world was loud, ugly to her. It hadn't felt that way to me, but maybe she was right.

Finally, she led me to where Sikari was working. Kaya knelt beside her and quietly started working, sharing the supplies my sister had laid out for us. I knelt beside them, the grain of the soil hard against my knees. Kaya grinned at me, laying her hand over mine to show me what to do.

As I worked beside them, I lost track of time, and I started when Kaya touched my hand, signalling me with an image of the rising sun. Light was appearing in the sky above us. I stood slowly, feeling the unexpected stiffness in my knees and back. So this was what work felt like. She touched me again, softly, a picture of myself, hands in the dirt, filling my vision. She was impressed.

As we rose into the air, I couldn't help but stare at the others, flying with us, their translucent wings shimmering in the rays of the rising sun. Lexi would love it. *Lexi.* Was I a traitor for having made it all night without seeing her face in my mind? Or were my thoughts betraying me now, bringing her image back to me when all I wanted to do was forget? Lexi, whose sight was so limited at night, whose skin thrived in the rays of the sun, who was most definitely a child of the day.

In the cool of the cave, alone in my room, I lay on my stomach in my bed. The household was silent; I missed the sound of the city lulling me to sleep. I blinked slowly and then, I was standing in the middle of a cornfield, looking at a small, red farmhouse on a flat plain. Somebody touched my shoulder, and, without looking, I knew who it was. Not because I read her thoughts; I didn't. I simply felt her. Lexi leaned her head softly on my shoulder, and I glanced down at her. She was older now, and her lips were turned up into a small, contented smile. The baby, cradled gently in her arms, slept, and curled up around the shoulder, just touching the edge of the fine, strawberry blonde hair, was the soft curve of a translucent wing.

When I opened my eyes again, it was night. I sat up, forcing myself to shake off the image of a life that could never be.

17

"Come," Teket said, gesturing for me to attack him again. The kid was relentless. He studied and worked in the fields now, but he saw his future clearly. He'd be a watchman. I moved towards him, crouching low like he'd shown me. "Come!" he shouted again. He'd been quicker at learning some of my phrases than I'd been at his. I had thought it would eventually be easy to feel at home. There was no more hiding. No more holding myself apart. No more watching from a distance. But as the days began to blend together, I found myself feeling almost as much an alien here as I had in my world before. I couldn't seem to learn the language. No, that wasn't quite true. I wasn't sure I was really trying. I came to recognize phrases and derive some meaning from conversations I overheard, but the effort was exhausting, and I stuck to reading thoughts.

Taking a breath, I readied myself. Teket had been teaching me how to fight – how to really fight – since I got here. Almost nightly, before my shift started, we'd meet at the small landing near our cave to train. He wanted to be a watchman, and he wanted his brother at his side.

I sprang, managing to grab his arm and twist it behind him.

He jerked his arm free and jabbed me in the ribs, swinging around and freeing his wrist from my grasp. I lunged towards him again, moving just in time to allow his blow to glance off my shoulder. I let my wings carry me up into the air and, even as he came up after me, I used the surge of wind to help me swing him around and force him, face down, onto the ground. He struggled, but keeping him pinned was easy. He'd been a good teacher. I wished I'd had his training before I was stabbed.

I got off Teket quickly, before I accidentally sent him my memory. He didn't need that in his head. He scrambled to his feet, grinning. "Good, good," he said, not minding the loss. He turned to face me again. "Come!" I obliged. I wasn't sure I wanted to be a watchman, but I wanted my brother to know that his dreams mattered. And since I didn't really have any of my own, his would have to suffice.

"Iuik!" Kaya called as I flew through the dark towards her. I was late, but, as always, she'd waited to go in. I'd lost track of time training with Teket. Training with him was invigorating. Working the earth with Kaya, though, was something else entirely.

She helped me more than she needed to, and working with her felt natural. I wondered, sometimes, if this wasn't what love was supposed to feel like: the slow, easy bloom of friendship.

I landed at the entrance and flashed her a grin. "Sorry," I said. She was familiar with the word by now and she smiled back at me. She took my hand and I followed her to the gardens. We were harvesting tonight. Of all the things we did together, gathering ripe produce was my favorite. They still did it by hand, like they did most things here.

Sakari waved at me from across the garden when she saw us. Nobody had done that before I'd come. Now it was a standard greeting between my family and me. Family. Even thinking the word was strange.

As Kaya and I moved down the quiet rows, her hand brushed against mine. As clear as if I'd thought it, I saw myself, in her mind, lean over and brush my lips against hers. The image was infused with the longing I felt in my own mind.

So what was stopping me? Kaya was beautiful. She was generous and sweet and open with her thoughts and feelings.

I turned away and I heard her sigh beside me. I knew it wasn't just the kiss. Kisses could wait. She wanted to know how I felt. How I really felt about her. But how could I give her that, when I wasn't even sure myself?

I didn't have to be reading her thoughts to know she was disappointed. Not just disappointed, though. Hurt. After a moment, I touched her hand again. I let her feel my emotions with me: confusion, sorrow, affection. She squeezed my hand but her mind was shut to me. I showed her a picture of her own hands through my eyes, the calm and patient way she tended the plants, her sure fingers as she pushed the seeds into the dirt. The way her eyes sparkled when she laughed. Warmth, now, from her. Forgiveness.

After a moment, she touched my hand, showing me an image of herself as a little girl: eyes bright, black hair just touching her shoulders. She remembered the scent of the dirt, how it drew her in. This was her calling. She showed me an image of myself now, working the earth along side of her. *Our calling.* She wanted me to see that I was her match, that I could love this earth and this moment and – her. And I wanted to. I pulled my hand away. I just couldn't find a way to convince my heart.

There were slight changes in the weather, but none so stark as in America. It was mostly just varying degrees of cold. I didn't mind it – my body thrived on the air and steady activity. As the seasons changed, Teket began to work outside in the fields more, and I joined him most of the time, instead of working the cave with Kaya. It was easier to think through my feelings when I wasn't around her all the time. She noticed and pulled away from me. I still caught her looking at me, but something between us changed. My stalled reaction, my withdrawal, had spoken more than words could have. Maybe that's what I liked about working with Teket. He was good at reminding me of the other options I had. Nik hadn't been exaggerating about how the girls here were beautiful, and Teket, at about fourteen, was all about pointing them out.

Teket looked up from the fence we were working on and tapped my arm, sending me the image of the girl opposite us, her back facing us as she wiggled around, digging out the snow that was packed in close to her tense legs. His hands stilled, the fence momentarily forgotten. I shot him a quick smile and continued tethering the pieces tightly together. He nudged me again and, when I met his gaze, he raised his eyebrows quizzically. I knew he wanted to know why none of his suggestions generated any interest. I shrugged, and he showed me an image of Kaya, her black eyes sparkling at me as she laughed. He wanted to know if she were the reason. I wanted her to be. If she were the reason nobody else interested me here, then my choice was easy. But if she were, why was I here with him instead of in the cave, kissing her?

I knew the answer, of course, even as I thought the question. How could any of these women compare to the girl with the changing eyes and the crazy hair and the spirit that fit so perfectly with mine? For the first time, I let him see my memories of Lexi. The way her hand fit in mine, the softness of her touch, how her eyes lit up when she looked at me. I showed him the curve of her lips when she smiled, and the cute way it turned down into the smallest, unintentional pout when she didn't get her way. I let him hear her voice as she sung for me and I allowed him to feel the way I felt when I had her in my arms, high above the world, allowing her to fly. I blinked the memory away, turning back to the fence.

He didn't say anything more; he just stood beside me quietly for a moment and then returned to working, his countenance downcast. Much later, when I thought about it, it occurred to me he had realized something at that moment I hadn't yet. This would never really be my home.

I should have been able to stay. It was where I belonged. I was with my family and others exactly like me. But none of it was good enough. It could have been, maybe, if Eric had found me before I found Lexi, but life doesn't always work out that way. No matter how much I was loved, it could never be home for me because it couldn't be home for Lexi. She *was* my home.

This new knowledge didn't hit me all at once, of course. It seeped in gradually: a general sense of dissatisfaction that always seemed to hang on me, the fact that I caught myself rehearsing ways to show my family I was leaving.

Maybe Lexi was the worst thing that ever happened to me. I pictured her mouth again. So much time had passed already. Would she want to see me? Would she be, like she'd said, waiting? Or had she moved on, met someone new, attributed everything that had happened with me to some strange fantasy. She must have left for college already. It wasn't as if we'd been together for long, although it felt like I'd known her forever. In reality, I had now been away from her longer than I had been with her. But it didn't change the fact that I couldn't pretend anymore that I would ever be satisfied without having her in my life. How could I leave my family, though, for a girl who might not even be there anymore? And how could I go back to being the person I was before?

"Iuik." My mother's quiet voice startled me as I stared up at the brightening sky from the entrance of the cave. She came to stand beside me, and I rested my hand on her shoulder. Instantly, her warmth flooded me. She'd missed me every day I'd been gone. I'd seen her memories by now, the ones where she wept over my blankets, where my father forgot his anger at her as he held her sobbing body, where each moment with her other two children felt incomplete because of my absence. But I rarely felt her grief from that time anymore, which is why I was startled when I felt a new, quiet sadness from her.

"What's wrong?" I asked. I turned to look at her, tilting my head. Lexi's face appeared, exactly as I'd shown my brother. He'd shown her.

"I won't go back," I said, focusing on my emotion when I'd been found by those children, on the overwhelming relief when I'd seen the love reflected in my mother's face, on how right it felt to be part of a family, part of this family.

"No, Iuik," she said, her words slow and careful. She repeated the image of Lexi again, and then envisioned me flying towards her. I knew she felt my sorrow, even as I fought against it. She was giving me permission to go.

"You don't understand. I can't go back to who I was." I couldn't keep it from her. And I couldn't go back to Lexi and pretend I didn't hate myself. Closing my eyes, I sent my mother the memories I was most ashamed of. I let her see me as I watched my marks, as I mapped out their routines, as I broke into their homes and took things I hadn't earned. I showed her how I watched violence and cruelty and did nothing – *nothing*. Hot tears streamed down my cheeks as the shame of who I was washed over me. She would know, now. She would hate me. She should hate me.

When I opened my eyes, she'd turned to face me. She lifted her arm and placed her hand on my cheek, looking into my eyes. "Iuik," she said, smiling gently. She mirrored an image I'd shown her of myself, walking through a darkened apartment, and replaced it with one I'd shown Teket of Lexi. The way Lexi looked at me left no room for argument; Lexi had known me – really known me – and she hadn't seen me as worthless at all. The image changed, and I could see myself now through my mother's eyes as I worked the soil along side of Sakari and outside with Teket, as we flew through the night together, hands joined. There was no condemnation in her emotions, and no repulsion. Only sorrow for me and an unwavering love. I shook my head. She couldn't understand…

As if she could hear the words in my thoughts, her scene shifted again. This time, I saw her, standing with Nik beside my sleeping, infant form in that valley. Her sense of regret was palpable. She'd lied to everyone to hide their relationship, and she had hidden her thoughts from her husband, denying the very thing that made their ability to communicate so beautiful. She knew shame.

The picture faded and I saw herself in her own mind, standing alone, half in shadows, half in light. Her eyes were downcast. Slowly, she lifted her chin, peering at first straight out in front of her. She began to shift her gaze skyward, her expression changing, from steady indifference to… hope. Light filtered down, slowly surrounding and enveloping her. I blinked. Somehow, her meaning was clear. Forgiveness. It wasn't her past that defined her.

The sentiment reminded me of Lexi and her story of the dragonfly. This hope for something bigger than ourselves and our own actions. "I love you," I said, knowing that, even though we didn't speak the same language, she could feel exactly what I meant.

She wrapped her arms around me and held me. I suddenly saw us embracing again, wrapped in a warm, shimmering light. We stood in the entrance together, in the warmth of the early morning sun, until my brother's arm touched mine. It was day.

18

My mother's message freed me to leave. I showed the rest of my family my intention that morning. The next night was bittersweet. As we ate breakfast together, we touched frequently, sharing the memories we'd made. This was our goodbye. I thought of Kaya. She would be hurt that I left without telling her – that I left at all. But she was beautiful and good. She would find a mate who could love her completely.

After breakfast, Sakari took my hand. Instead of taking me to the growing caves, she flew me around the perimeter of our village. Leaving, we knew, was forbidden. Nik had had to remove his wings in order to leave; I'd seen what that had done to him, how bitterness and hatred had twisted his whole person. I didn't intend to do the same.

She took me out to the ledge where the children found me, the night I'd gotten here. The skies were empty. Empty, but not unpatrolled. Sakari touched me, and I saw the watchmen, flying low with weapons poised. The image evaporated.

Back at home, my mother showed me the rest of the plan. I would leave the comfortable sandals behind, trading them for the sneakers I'd worn here. They were more durable and better for my intended trek through the snow. I'd also leave behind the tunics I'd grown so accustomed to wearing, aside from the white one I would wear. Instead, I would take my black shirt and rough black denim with me. I'd gotten used to the softened wool tunics worn by my people and the freedom of movement that loose cloth allowed; I wasn't looking forward to the restricting trappings of my former attire. Alone in my room, I slowly placed my black clothing inside my bag, rolling it tight so I could fill the rest of the space with a small canteen of water and the food my mother had prepared for me. I brought the pack to her, and she took it, brushing my fingers with hers as she did. Hope and despair co-mingled.

My brother came out of his room and stopped me before I returned to mine. He quickly threw his arms around me. He stifled a sob in my chest and I held him close, placing my hand on his hair.

When he finally let me go, I walked quickly to my room, careful not to look back. I took off my tunic and laid it on the bed, getting under the warm blankets and staring, wide awake, at the wall.

It was next to impossible for me to sleep during the night but, somehow, I had my first dreamless sleep since I'd arrived there. When the light of day dawned, I was up with the sun. The cave was quiet; I'd asked my family to stay sleeping while I left. I didn't want them to be implicated in my defection. I also didn't want to be reminded of reasons to change my mind. I stood in front of the heavy, brown curtain for a long time, my fingers running along the familiar texture. I slowly moved it aside and stepped into the main area of the still cave. I made my way to the mouth. The day workers had already begun their shifts, and the watchmen would be patrolling from the east. This was it. As I walked around to the north of the mountain, I scanned the skies again. Empty. Then, keeping my body parallel to the face of the mountain, so close I could have reached out and touched it with my fingertips, I flew down, swiftly and single-mindedly. I had to pace myself, though. Whenever I began moving too quickly, my ears started to feel full and then I was forced to stop and allow my body to adjust to the change in elevation. The air became warmer, less comforting. It took me much of the day to put enough distance between my home and me to feel confident that I wouldn't be easily spotted. The only way they would find me was if they went looking deliberately and, chances were, I wouldn't be missed right away. Finally, I could see the white earth below. Staying low, I continued to fly along the ground. I should have felt completely alone but, even as I created distance between my family and myself, I felt their warmth; it was a tangible, unmistakable sensation.

As the sky darkened, I forced myself to slow my flight, landing carefully in the thin covering of snow. It took a moment to get used to the feeling of solid ground beneath my feet and another to steady my legs. I set out quickly and quietly, walking close to the tree line, hoping my shoe prints wouldn't reveal my presence to the search party that would, undoubtedly, be sent out. I hadn't used my legs for any distance since I'd arrived and, after a few hours, my calves were cramping. I forced my body to walk through the pain. As the night neared its end, it took controlled effort not to cry out with every step. Finally, just before dawn, I pulled myself into a small cropping of trees and collapsed against one of them, panting with the effort. They would be ending the main search effort soon, but members of the watch would still be looking. I slept very little, despite my physical exhaustion and, by the first rays of dawn, I was up on my feet again, walking through the snow, my muscles screaming in protest.

I walked for three more days, until my body knew it was time. I felt my wings responding to the environment around me. My wings, alive again, carried me high above the ground at last, far from the hard earth. Being in the air so often and so freely had given me a new strength, and I found I had endurance I'd never known before. My wings didn't tire, and I went as far as I could during the day and well into the night; the darkness, like a familiar caress, welcomed me back into its embrace.

As I approached the populated areas and then the Russian cities, I flew only at night. I'd betrayed my people by leaving, but I wouldn't betray them by being caught. As soon as I reached the first city, I changed back into my fitted black attire. I stuck to the rooftops, to the unpopulated areas, or to those places so riddled with crime and decay that nobody would notice me there. This time, when my food ran out, I went without for as long as I could and then turned to gathering at city dumps and in farmers' fields. I spent this first part of my return sick, as a result. The adjustment from the natural diet of my family to the one I found necessary was painful and unpleasant. But I marvelled at how much easier the trip was, now that my wings were stronger. I pictured my mother and siblings. Would they have to grieve for me again? Or would they, like me, feel our connection even over the miles between us?

Eventually, I could feel myself nearing my destination. The air was different, and my body knew I would soon be there. I'd thought, at first, that I would go right to Lexi but, somewhere along the way, I realized I needed to make a stop first. Gradually it came into view. The large expanse of empty field and the modest house near the end of the long gravel driveway called to me. Nik's place. I had to be sure he was still there, that he hadn't gone after Eric or Lexi. I landed softly in the field and, folding my wings tight against my body, walked up towards the house. If he were there, I didn't want to give him any warning. I looked out, as I went, at what appeared to be an endless expanse of grass and grain. There were no houses for miles, and his property stretched far enough to render the fences marking its boundaries invisible to me from my vantage point. I pictured tall trees planted along the edges, providing privacy during the day, and, with no close neighbours to light up the sky, darkness concealing me at night. If I had land like this – I didn't allow myself to finish the thought. Slowing, quietly, I pushed open the door and went inside.

There was a faint smell – of musty, unused furniture perhaps. I cautiously made my way down the hall to Nik's room. No movement. It seemed he was gone. As I entered his room, I saw immediately that he had indeed left and that his departure was permanent. Skeletal remains were all that was left of Nik on this earth. The window, partially ajar, had let enough of the wildlife in to speed up his decay; any tissue that may have been left to testify to his humanity had long since been carried away. The bones were scattered across the bed and onto the floor. I sat on the bed beside what looked like his thorax. He may have hated me and nearly everything else on this side of the world, but he had truly loved my mother. I lifted it up, mildly surprised by its weight and lack of brittleness, and looked closer. On the underside were four notched markings where the wings would have been. Our wings grew from bone; they were an integral part of our makeup. I gently put it back down on the bed.

Maybe I should have been more conflicted than I was, wondering if I'd done the right thing, leaving the safety and freedom of my home and not honoring his final wishes. But I wasn't worrying about that at all. Instead, I was trying to decide whether or not I needed to bury him and looking, with curiosity, at the edge of a large manila envelope peeking out from under his pillow. Was it morbid, sitting here beside his bones, reading his mail? Couldn't be any worse than picking up parts of his skeleton. I pulled the envelope out and turned it over in my hands. It wasn't mail at all. It was unsealed and unlabelled. It had belonged to Nik.

I opened it and slid out the contents. Several deeds. My name was on all of them. If I could find a way to sell the properties,

I could live on the proceeds. Money would never have to be an issue. As I flipped through, I stopped at the one for the farmhouse. A yellow note was paper clipped to the top. Nik's almost illegible scrawl was unmistakable.

Joshua – If you didn't make it home, you can stay here if you want. Place is paid for, after all. That was all. No parting insights, last epiphanies, not even a final salutation. But it was a goodbye, nevertheless. What would I do in a place like this? Was it far enough from the neighbouring farms to make any flight feasible? Or was he, by offering me this place, sentencing me to be locked on the land like he'd been?

I buried him then, carving a wooden marker from the frame of the bed. I burnt the rest of the bed; Nik had died in it and I didn't want it, especially if I were thinking of making this place liveable. And I realized, as I watched the flames devour the soiled bed, that I might be. Whether or not Lexi would have me, I could live here if I needed to. It was far enough from the rest of the world, with a large enough piece of property to allow for privacy and, besides, it reminded me of home – both the home I grew up in and the one I returned to. It reminded me of Goodnight Moon and goodnight kisses, of hugs and games, of working the land with my sister. I imagined Lexi and I years in the future, sitting by the large fireplace, my arm around her shoulders and her small frame tucked in close to mine. Not that we'd need to settle here, but we could. I reminded myself of a truth that Nik had taught me long ago. Wishes are for fools and children. But it didn't stop me, this time, from wishing.

The fire smouldered outside, and I stood in front of the large, square mirror in the bathroom. Using Nik's razor, I carefully shaved, slowly seeing the old me returning. As I looked into my own face, smooth and familiar, I felt shame wash over me. "I'm sorry," I whispered aloud. Before me was the man who had spent his life stealing from people, who had watched suffering and pain and had felt nothing, done nothing. This was the man who consistently left the only people who loved him. And somehow, this same man was planning to go back to Lexi. How could I possibly expect her to want a life with me?

Dragonfly, I heard her voice in my mind, feeling her certainty and faith again. She didn't care who I'd been. Neither, I realized, did my family. That's what love did. I thought again of the image of my mother, surrounded in light. The unwavering hope she had. I closed my eyes, shutting out my reflection, focusing only on the faith they'd been showing me. *I'm so sorry*, I whispered again. A slow warmth washed over me and I exhaled deeply. I opened my eyes and blinked quickly, turning from the mirror. I might look like the man I was, but I wasn't him anymore.

19

I spent the next two nights cleaning. I was pretty sure it was a stalling technique. But I scrubbed the floor, and I washed and dried and pressed the sheets and bedding for the small room Lexi and I had shared that night. I did the dishes and wiped down the walls. As I fell into bed with the sun, I couldn't help but wonder if I'd end up coming back here alone after all. I comforted myself with the fact that even perpetual bachelors could use a clean floor.

When I finally set out towards Lexi, I breathed the sky air deeply. The trip was infinitely nicer than it was in the confines of a car. I could see the landscape change, not just its climate but also the shape and texture of the terrain. It was amazing. The drawback, as always, was finding areas to rest, since the journey, even with my newfound flight speed, took days. I stopped to sleep only when my body refused to give any more, and tall hotel rooftops along the way served my purposes well enough.

It gave me time to think, though. Even if Lexi still wanted me, how could I possibly ask her to leave her family? I'd had to choose. But maybe she didn't. Not yet, at any rate. I didn't want Lexi to leave everything for me. I didn't want to tear her away from her family, without them ever knowing why. And I didn't want to fly away to some selfish existence. I wanted us both to be happy. I pictured the New York skyline again, in all its brightly lit beauty. I'd used the dark as cover for obscurity and theft. Maybe I could use it for something else. The last time I'd tried to rescue someone, I'd nearly been killed. But that had been on impulse. No planning, no equipment. No training. I'd be prepared next time. *Next time.* It was insane to even think it. But somehow, it felt right. Teket had trained me as a watchman. Those months, learning how to defend and attack, honing my strength and speed, equipping myself to use my wings in battle, hadn't been a loss. I'd called myself a villain, but maybe I didn't need to be one.

As I flew, the remnants of winter remained and the cool weather reminded me, pleasantly, of home in the caves. As I neared her city, I felt my palms begin to sweat. It had been so long. Even if she were still there, it had been over a year since we'd last seen each other. What would I say to her?

I arrived in the city as night was ending and I realized I had no idea what day it was. I reviewed my options. I had very few, and the sky would soon be light. I went to the only place I could think of; I returned to my small, derelict apartment. I'd left the screenless window open, and I entered quickly. Home, for now. As I walked towards the small kitchen area, I looked around; it was dark, as usual, except for a small tea light set up in the middle of the table. It was lit. I froze. My heart thudded in my ears. Stupid, stupid, stupid. Slowly, I stepped backwards.

"You're here." Marcus' gravelled voice broke through my blind fear and I almost laughed in relief as he rose from the couch.

"Marcus!" I wasn't sure I'd ever been so grateful to see anyone as I was to see him. "I didn't realize you'd be here!"

"You hadn't been back for a while, so I didn't know when to expect you. I've been checkin' our spot still. An' it was getting' cold in my old place. I thought – heck, if this place's good enough for

Joshua, it'll be good enough for me." He limped towards the table. "Like what I done with the place?"

"It's great."

"Want it pretty. It should be presentable when my girl and the kids get back." A new story. "But if you need me ta clear out, I can be packed in a little minute. You can even keep the candle."

"No. It's great Marcus. It's a great place for you."

"Well, you're welcome to stay here with me. Haven't had a roommate for years. Might be kinda nice."

"Thanks for the invitation. I might take you up on it."

"Hope you do." Marcus opened the cupboard. "Hungry?"

"I am." I watched curiously as he pulled out a half-loaf of bread and a small jar of strawberry jam. Placing two pieces of bread on the counter in front of him, he spread on the jam with a tarnished but clean butter knife.

"Been working," he said as he brought the bread over. He placed one piece in front of me and took one for himself, sitting down across from me. He gestured towards a small, plastic bucket and a squeegee propped up against the wall by the door. "Been washin' windows. People waitin' at lights always appreciate a clean window."

"That's great. Really great." I meant it.

"Real glad to have some company," he said, sounding almost warm.

"Me too."

"So, what's your next move?" he asked me, his mouth full.

I imagined myself telling him about my trip home, about my family, about my decision. Instead, I asked, "Remember that girl?"

"'Course. The gullible one."

I smiled at his description and then couldn't help but be serious again. "I came to see if she'd still have me."

"Well, that's great, I guess." He hesitated. "Do you think she can be trusted?"

"I think so. I'm willing to give it a shot, if she'll let me."

"Well, be careful," he said. He looked like he wanted to say something else but changed his mind.

"Always am."

After we had finished our meager meal, he rose and put the remaining loaf, with the tightly sealed jam, back into the cupboard.

I watched as he began preparing to work. He added soap to his empty bucket, which he planned to fill in the fountain down the street, and then he grabbed his squeegee. "See you later, Joshua," he said, as he headed out the door.

"Marcus," I said, stopping him. "What day is it today?"

He shook his head at me. "You really have been gone a long time." As he pulled the door shut, he said, "Thursday."

Thursday. I couldn't have asked for better timing. It made everything suddenly more real, more urgent. The light, as usual, imprisoned me.

I forced myself to lie down. My body didn't care that I'd been up for days before this or that I needed to rest before what could be the most disappointing moment of my life. All I could think about was Lexi.

The quiet click of the door woke me, and I saw Marcus setting down the half empty bucket, after ringing out the squeegee. He walked softly to the kitchen table, where he lit the candle, emptied his pockets, and began counting his change. I glanced immediately at the window; it was dark. Sitting, I asked, "What time is it?"

"Anxious to see your lady?"

"Yes." There was no sense denying it.

"Well, not sure for sure. But the time on the bank sign when I passed it a while back said nine." Nine. Her folks would be gone. She might be too, but I couldn't really ask for a more opportune time. "Well, go get your girl," he said, after the silence began to stretch.

"Okay. How do I look?"

"Stealthy," he said, eyeing my tight black shirt and fitted jeans. Was he being funny? The corners of his lips turned up into the smallest hint of a smile. Marcus had made a joke. No matter what else happened, that in and of itself was a small miracle. "See you, Joshua."

"See you, Marcus." And then, I was up in the air again, allowing my wings finally to take me, as fast as they could, to Lexi's. The rooftop across from Lexi's apartment seemed to be waiting for me. I'd spent so much time there, first when I was studying my mark and later when I was watching Lexi.

I set down and peered through the darkness at the living room window. There was no movement, and I felt the quick sting of rejection. What did I expect? I continued to watch until my shoulders ached from being so still.

Finally, a soft light came on in her room. The lamp. She opened the curtains, and I saw her clearly. Bright pink hair, cut into a bob. I suspected her eyes would be a wild color, too, and I wished I could see them from where I stood. She reached out and put her palm against the glass, leaning forward and resting her forehead against it too. She pulled the glass open, and then, looking out for a long moment again, turned away and disappeared into her room. I could picture her sliding into bed, pulling the covers over her body. Without thinking, I rose into the air, allowing myself to be carried over the street far below and to her window. As I got there, I noticed that the curtain was moving very slightly with the breeze. On impulse, I reached out. No screen.

She'd left the window open for me. She'd kept her promise, with a weird, unshakable confidence in my ability not to disappoint. I moved the curtains gently and, as I did, she turned her head and opened her eyes. She looked at me, blinking slowly at first, and then she gasped and sat up straight. She was wearing the blue nightshirt again. I smiled in at her as she shook her head in amazement. "Weren't you expecting me?" I forced my tone to be light, teasing.

"You're really not a dream." Clapping her hands together suddenly, she threw her head back and laughed. "I knew you'd come!" Shoving the covers off her lap, off the bed, she ran to the window. She hugged me frantically through the window and then, impulsively, lifted herself through, thrusting herself out into my arms, trusting me entirely. I surprised myself by being unfazed. She was no burden at all in my arms, and I lifted her easily above her apartment and landed, still holding her, on her rooftop. I set her gently down, and she grabbed hold of both of my hands in hers, looking up intently into my face. "You really came back for me."

"How could I not? You were right."

"I usually am," she said. She slid her arms around my neck. "Are you going to say it, my sweet dragonfly?"

"Say what? That you're right? I already did."

"No, the other thing. The reason you came back."

"Oh, that," I said. I didn't even hesitate. "I love you. You're where I belong."

She answered me by pressing her lips against mine, part passion and part tenderness. She pulled away slightly, whispering against my mouth, "Me too. To all of it."

We stood in embrace, looking out into the city before us, my arms wrapped tightly around her body and hers around mine. Finally, she broke the silence. "So, what now?

"What now?" Whatever the future held, we'd face it together. There was no rush. I looked down at the city, the light from below illuminating the dark. "Anything's possible, Lexi. The sky's the limit."

www.ingramcontent.com/pod-product-compliance
Lightning Source LLC
Chambersburg PA
CBHW020548310726
48979CB00008B/1138/J
* 9 7 8 1 9 8 8 2 7 6 0 5 2 *